Chopstix

A. T. Raydan

"Our greatest glory is not in never falling,

but in rising every time we fall."

(Confucius)

Unique Inspiration

creativity • uniquely inspired

First published in 2015 by Unique Inspiration,

Ground Floor, Fort Dunlop, Fort Parkway, Birmingham,

West Midlands. B24 9FE. United Kingdom

www.uniqueinspiration.co.uk

Chopstix by A. T. Raydan

Cover Illustrated by Elena Ferroli

© Unique Inspiration Limited, 2015

All rights reserved

PB ISBN: 978-1-907525-19-3

ePub ISBN: 978-1-907525-29-2

A CIP catalogue record for this book is available from the British Library.

15 14 7 6 5 4 3 2 1

Printed and bound in Great Britain by Clays Ltd, St Ives plc.

Unique Inspiration

creativity • uniquely inspired

Love you, Always

xxxx

Prologue

I arrived at the old bank and witnessed the robbery first hand. Once again, my instincts had guided me to a dangerous situation, where a crime was being committed.

I knelt down on the roof of the building opposite the bank and looked towards it. Two men dressed uniformly in black from head to toe, were carrying a large black holdall from the bank towards their car. They were struggling as they lifted it and placed it into the boot of their car. Then, they rushed back into the bank. They seemed determined and on a mission.

I looked around and there was no one to be seen. There was an eerie silence. It was a warm night, with clear skies yet it was very dark near the bank. There were no lights on around me and it was as though somehow they had managed to bypass the banks security systems too. The alarms had not been triggered and these individuals didn't look like bank staff. They looked very serious.

A few minutes later, two of them emerged with another holdall. Once again they appeared to be struggling with it.

I could no longer wait. I put on my mask and prepared myself. This was not like my previous encounters. I feared that they might be armed, especially as they were carrying out such a serious crime.

My heart and mind were aligned and for once, I was ready.

"Stop!" I shouted down from the roof, as they prepared to load the second holdall into their car.

The men looked startled and they dropped the holdall. As it landed on the floor, a wad of bank notes fell out. I was right. I had just disturbed a bank robbery. The robbers hadn't even attempted to hide their faces. Were they that confident of getting away with the crime they had planned to commit or were they being arrogant?

One of the men looked up towards me and started shouting obscenities, whilst flexing his muscles. Initially I feared the worst, but then remembered one of fathers Confucian principles, 'Wherever you go, go with all your heart'. There was no going back. I was ready.

I slowly rose to my feet, turned around and took a few steps backwards so that I was out of sight.

"Get out of here!" shouted one of the men.

"Leave her, let's finish the job and get out of here," I overheard his accomplice say.

They started to lift the holdall again with a view to placing it into their car.

I stood up feeling tall and strong. I looked around and evaluated my options. The building closest to me would provide the perfect platform. I took a running leap off the roof on to the roof of the building beside me, which was lower in height. As I landed, I rose again and continued with another running leap off the roof. I landed on the grass verge with a forward roll, and assumed a low crouched position with one hand firmly on the floor. The second hand was by my side.

"This is your final warning," I shouted across to the men.

They looked stunned and once again they dropped the holdall. This seemed to anger them. Clearly, they were not in the mood to just give up.

It left me with no choice. I got up and ran towards one of the men as fast as I could. As I neared him, I knocked him to the ground using a low sweep kick. He wasn't expecting it and I had caught him by surprise.

The second robber ran for cover, or rather I thought that's what he was doing. But it was at that point when I realised what I had got myself into. He turned, pulled out a gun and aimed it directly towards me. Without warning, he fired. I jumped up and performed a backwards flip. As I landed, I reached for my own weapon of choice. I drew a chopstick, took aim and threw it towards him. It hit him directly on his hand forcing him to drop the gun. They were no ordinary chopsticks. But that was just a temporary reprieve.

Without hesitation, I took out a second chopstick and ran towards him. As I edged closer I met him with a front kick at full force, dropping him to the floor in the process. Only, he managed to grab my ankle as he fell. This was unplanned and unexpected. I lost my balance and started to fall. I had to react quickly and do something, as otherwise I would be in serious trouble. Instinct took over enabling me to swing my arm and stab him in the leg with my chopstick.

Blood began to spurt out of his leg and he started to scream in agony. Aunt Daiyu was right, the chopsticks were very sharp and could pierce anything. I pulled out the chopstick and moved away from him.

All of a sudden, I heard the sound of someone running towards me. As I turned around I saw a third robber, but it was too late. He leapt for me, tackling me to the ground. As I landed, I banged my head on the floor and grazed my arm. He was on top of me.

He reached for a knife and pointed it towards me. I had no choice but to defend myself again. I held my chopstick firmly and slashed his cheek with it. There was no reaction from him as I drew blood. A scuffle followed, and I dropped my chopstick. He too dropped the knife that he was carrying. I had to think back to all that my parents had taught me about the art of self-defence in order to free myself from him.

As I broke free, I noticed a tattoo on his neck.

"Who are you and what does that sign on your neck mean?" I gasped.

He remained unmoved by my question and didn't reply. Instead he just stared at me and smiled. Suddenly, I felt two arms grab me around my waist. It was the first robber again. He wrapped his arms around me tightly and started to squeeze.

His accomplice, whom I had just slashed across the face stood up. He was very, very angry. His eyes were popping out of their sockets.

"It's time we stopped playing games. You do not realise the damage you have caused tonight," he said, as he walked over towards his knife.

He picked it up and headed for me. He was angry and I feared the worst. As he neared me, I lifted up my legs and kicked him in his chest. I used his chest to flip myself up backwards and over his accomplice who was gripping me. As I made it over I used my legs to kick his legs from under me.

I noticed both of my chopsticks on the floor and immediately reached for them.

Now it was my turn.

I moved towards both of the robbers. They were rooted to the spot. As I neared them, I crossed my arms and slashed them across their chests. I had cut through their clothes and inflicted injuries to both of them.

I fell to the ground and reached for their ankles, pulling them and knocking them to the ground in the process. I needed to stop them and had no other option than to stab them with the chopsticks. I aimed for the back of their ankles and took aim with a chopstick in each hand.

They both screamed in agony, more so, when I pulled the chopsticks out.

I had incapacitated all three of them. I had a look at their necks and noticed that each one had the same distinct tattoo.

All of a sudden I could hear police sirens in the distance. I needed to move fast. I put my chopsticks away, turned to the robbers and spoke,

"Justice is served."

I then ran towards the building opposite and disappeared into the alley. I climbed up the scaffolding on the side of the building and as I reached the top, I lay low awaiting the arrival of the police.

It was at that moment that I noticed that my lungs were screaming and my heart was beating so hard that I thought it would burst out of my chest.

I noticed drops of blood on the floor. I was clearly bleeding. I had grazed my arm earlier when I was floored by one of the men. I also had cuts to my arm and my face.

The police arrived and set about trying to make sense of what they found. It didn't take them long to figure out what had happened when they found the bags of money. They apprehended the robbers. I reflected on what happened out there tonight. For the first time in my life, I had inflicted injury to others. This wasn't me.

Who am I?

I was never like this. Fate had dealt me a cruel blow and carved me a new path to follow.

In life there are alienated individuals that have a strong hatred of life. This causes them to forget who they really are and their purpose in life.

I always believed those individuals were selfish, self-centred and egotistical. The epitome of what I never wished to be.

I could never understand what drove those individuals to become like this. That is, until the day that I too became one of them.

Who am I...?

First Day at College

It was October 6th and my first day at college. It was a bright sunny day and not raining for once. Perfect, I thought, as I had my hair especially done for the occasion and even treated myself to a new outfit. It was a pink dress, with a straight cut and formal fit. And my shoes? Yes, they were new too. Pink shoe boots to be precise, with an open toe. Why the new outfit? I don't know. I guess I just felt that with it being a new college, new start, perhaps it was time for a new me. After all, I wasn't the type of girl to draw attention towards myself. I was just plain simple Wendy, Wendy Wu, that's me.

I was born right here in this great city, New Valliant City, whereas my parents, they were born and raised in

China, Zhejiang province to be precise, or if you're like me, you'll refer to it as Shanghai. I was never able to get away with calling it Shanghai as it somehow always offended my father.

My father was very proud of his roots. I always felt that emotionally and spiritually he was still connected to Zhejiang. He always will be.

He was a proud man, boasting about how Zhejiang produced one-third of China's sea crustaceans thanks to its long irregular coastline. Apparently, it was a rich haven for crabs, prawns and shrimps. Now I'm beginning to sound boring, so let me stop right there, after all, we don't want to get off on the wrong foot, do we?

My fathers love of food and the location of his birthplace meant that there was only ever one dream that he wanted to fulfil. To own a chain of authentic Chinese restaurants, first right here and then in every city he could think of. Sounds ambitious? Well, my father was the type to be just that. He was very thorough and he always did his homework. He had already managed to open his first restaurant and make that a huge success.

Recently he had been to quite a few franchise seminars to work out how he could expand and start to realise his dream. When it came to the art of perfection, my father was an expert.

I'm not sure whether my mother shared the same dream or whether she was driven in the same way, but she never said otherwise. She never spoke out against my father, not on anything.

Both my parents had quite a tough upbringing and they emigrated before I was born. I have never truly understood why they left their roots, everything they owned and all that they knew, for a new life right here. They had started afresh and rebuilt their lives completely.

Whilst they both spoke English, it was rather basic and just about sufficient at the time for them to get by. Since then, well, let's just say they blend in well now. At home, they occasionally break into a little mandarin too, although a lot less now than when I was younger. Maybe that was just so as to encourage me to learn it? I don't know. I'm second-guessing now.

When I questioned why they uprooted, all I was told is that they wanted the best possible upbringing for me. Why wasn't Shanghai good enough? I would love to travel there now. Have you ever seen the images of Shanghai on television or in a magazine? Amazing, awe-inspiring, stunning are just some of the words that spring to mind when describing it.

I don't know any different. I guess I'll never truly appreciate what it's like to leave all you know behind in order to restart your life in some alien place where you barely speak the language.

Deep down, I knew that college was the beginning of the long road towards making my parents proud of me, by achieving the best grades that I could. Maybe one day I too would understand the sacrifices that my parents made. More about my family later, it's my first day at college remember.

So, there I was, enrolment day at college, the day when you select the subjects you'd like to study as well as the social groups that you'd like to join. It was one of the top colleges around, where all the smart, well-spoken and rich kids went. My parents weren't rich, but I'd like to think that I was well spoken and sort of smart. I always aimed for the top grades in all of my subjects. My parents encouraged and drove me to be that way.

So, what am I studying? English Literature, History, Law and Psychology. My chosen subjects would serve me well in order to help me realise my career ambitions. I longed to be a lawyer and one day own my own firm. I figured that psychology would help me understand the mindset and behaviour of people. I was looking forward to it.

I didn't join any social groups, as I figured that bit could wait for a while.

There were a handful of students from my last school that were also due to start at college today, but I had decided not to socialise with them and to make a fresh start.

Well, okay, so that's not quite true. To be honest, I didn't really have many friends at school. I was too serious a student to have friends. Guys often saw me as a challenge and I was usually at the centre of many wind-ups, usually around who could successfully ask me out. No one ever succeeded. As for the girls, well, apart from a few, I found most of them too immature for my liking and I wasn't one for the silly childish mind games they liked to play.

At college, my intention was to keep a low profile yet no fewer than seven guys had already tried to introduce themselves to me.

What is it with guys? Each one used the same cheesy chat up lines with me and these were no different to the ones used during my school days. Maybe that's partly the reason that I was still single.

As for the girls, well, they were being girls. No doubt, looking at my clothes, perhaps my shoes too and making judgment about me without even getting to know me. Maybe it was down to my exotic looks or my dress sense, hey it could be down to a million and one reasons. I always attracted unwarranted attention of girls for one reason or another.

It wasn't the case that I was the only oriental girl around. In fact, there were quite a few. And then there were the French girls, Indian girls and even Spanish girls.

At school, it was the same. I always wanted to be different in every way. Not exciting, just different. Not following any fashion trends or any trends to be honest. I guess I just wanted to be myself.

I never truly figured out how you dealt with other girls. Does anyone in life?

I was always taught to love one another, yet others were more geared up to love themselves with a zest for mischief making, spreading lies or vicious rumours and then watching on as others were hurt or humiliated.

I'm grateful to my mother for my exotic looks, elegance and simplicity. I know I haven't spoken about her much but she truly is my role model.

I know, the first women we learn from are usually our mothers and that the first role model for how we want to be as a woman in the world is usually our mother and I'm no different there.

Between you and me, she's someone I aspired to be like in every aspect, from her charm, sensuality, elegance to her inner assertive self. My friends quite often commented on how well spoken I was but to me, it was the only way I knew, thanks to my mother.

I learned kindness, acceptance, and open-mindedness from my mother. She showed her emotions, including her love and affection for my father and me. I saw her cry when she was hurt, and smile and laugh when she was happy.

More about my mother later. The guys and girls at college, yes, that's where we were. And then, along came Andre. I remember our first ever conversation very well.

"Nice dress," said Andre.

"Thanks," I replied.

He was different, a cute kind of different. He didn't comment on my looks and actually noticed my dress. Do you know how long it took me to find a dress that I liked? He would've received higher marks if he commented on my shoes, but the dress wasn't a bad start.

I smiled, "I'm Wendy, Wendy Wu," I said.

Andre smiled too. He had a magnetism of sorts. The positive kind, I think. I can't explain it. Girls would understand what I mean.

"I'm Andre, delighted to meet you," he replied.

Wow, a French sounding name with a polite English accent. I was naturally drawn to him and that was just not how I was.

"First day?" he asked.

"Mmm hmmm," I replied, nodding.

And so began our friendship. It was a simple start, but simplicity has a degree of elegance attached to it.

Don't get me wrong, I for one never liked flirting with guys. But, Andre was different and came across as a gentleman. First impressions? He stood head and shoulders above everyone else. I liked that.

Enrolment took a few hours, with every subject head trying to convince me that his or her subject was more important than anyone else's. Think of it as going to the supermarket and the manufacturer of every cereal trying to convince you that theirs was the healthiest and the best. Only this was happening in college.

Anyway, I managed a whole day without bumping into someone from my old school, which was great. It meant that we weren't in the same classes and I'd have the opportunity to be myself.

After completing enrolment, Andre offered to buy me a drink. Before you jump to any conclusions, it was the non-alcoholic type. I don't drink. Well, not yet anyway.

I agreed and off we strolled to Bar Chocolato, his choice, not mine. I hadn't even had time to get my bearings yet.

Bar Chocolato was a cosy café with a distinct chocolate theme. The wallpaper was like a giant chocolate wrapper. It was purple and brown in colour with an embossed foil effect. Some would call the décor tacky, but not me. I'll stick up for all things chocolate each and every time.

There were a dozen or so tables in the café, all close to one another. The tables were fairly low and the chairs were round, soft and very comfy. It was lively in there with the buzz of various conversations taking place and the occasional burst of laughter.

Looking around, I noticed a few tables of singletons too, reading away whilst enjoying a drink and a slice of cake. I could see myself spending a lot of time in here.

"What can I get you?" asked Andre.

I spent a few seconds browsing the menu and responded, "I'll try the Bar Chocolato Special".

"Whipped cream and extra chocolate?" asked Andre.

I pondered for a few milliseconds…

"Sure, the more chocolate and whipped cream the merrier," I replied, giving away my weakness for chocolate straight away.

"I guarantee that this will be the best chocolate drink you've ever tasted," said Andre.

He was very sure of himself, in a firm, commanding and authoritative way.

We sat down and waited for our drinks to arrive. There was a strange silence for what seemed like a few minutes. But as it started to reach the uncomfortable stage, our drinks arrived. Phew, that was close, I thought to myself.

As I took my first sip of the Bar Chocolato Special, I realised that Andre was right.

It was lusciously rich with a smooth nutty chocolatey flavour. I'm beginning to sound like a food critic now. I decided to keep that to myself; after all, I didn't want him to get ahead of himself with a compliment so early in our friendship.

The conversation switched to education, aspirations and ambitions.

Wow, intellectual conversation over a delightful hot chocolate drink, the perfect combination. Was this guy for real? I asked myself.

I was a very private person as I was the defensive type, always trying to work out motives before I let my guard down. But, in a strange way, I was able to be myself with someone I had only just met. I was relaxed but a little apprehensive. This had never happened to me before.

Education, aspirations and ambitions, yes, that's what we were talking about.

"I'd like to follow a career in law. A lawyer with my own firm one day," I replied.

Andre smiled.

"That sounds cool," he said.

"What about you?" I asked.

"I'm not sure what I'd like to be, an engineer perhaps, maybe a research scientist or even a computer programmer," replied Andre.

"Let me get through college and when it's time to decide on university, I'll tell you then," continued Andre, whilst smiling.

"I love exploring how things work. In fact, I'm always experimenting and inventing new things in my workshop, just last week I made a miniature GPS tracker for my cats collar. I can now find her when she gets lost," added Andre.

I'll take back what I said about him being authoritative and sure. In some aspects, he was still a guy, unsure about what he wanted from life.

We spoke for well over an hour, although at the time it felt like a few minutes. As it approached 4pm, I started to make a move, as I needed to be home to help with my parents business. Andre seemed disappointed that I was leaving. He definitely liked me.

"Thanks for the drink. You were right, it's definitely the best chocolate drink I've had," and then I paused for a few seconds, before I added, "Next time, it's on me".

"Sure, I'll hold you to that," replied Andre excitedly and almost immediately.

We went our separate ways. I headed to the bus stop. It was one of those days when everything ran like clockwork. No sooner had I arrived at the bus stop, a bus pulled up. I boarded the bus and started to think about my day, after all it was an eventful first day at college. Seven guys trying to hit on me, catty looks from other girls and a guy that appeared mature beyond his years, so polite and well spoken.

It wasn't like me to just agree to a drink with anyone. I was the cautious type. My parents had taught me to be that way. Yet, today felt so natural and so right.

Something told me that college would be fun and provide me with the platform to help me fulfil my potential in life.

My stop arrived and I got off. Home was only a few minutes' walk away and I knew my parents would ask about college. Just enough time to work out what I tell them and more importantly, what I don't.

I never kept secrets from my parents and I never once felt the urge to do so as I knew they always had my best interests at heart.

My parents were very strict. Having guys as friends was always challenging as they both felt that I needed to be careful as guys are usually only after one thing. Friendship, maybe? No, not according to my parents! Generally, I tended to agree with them.

I guess they had strong cultural and traditional values too. Either way, they were very protective of me and that was a reflection of how much they loved me. I may have found their views a bit old fashioned at times but I could never go against them.

They will use quotes from the great and the good to explain most things in life. Something like 'The parents age must be remembered, both for joy and anxiety'.

I think I know what that meant...

The House of Wu

I arrived home. Well, it was my home, but to others, it was the House of Wu. That was the name of the family restaurant, my parents pride and joy.

It was my parents first ever restaurant and the foundation of the future franchise aspirations that they had in mind.

I quickly changed and headed to find my mother. She was in charge of taking all of the bookings. I needed to know the names of the guests for the day.

No, I wasn't planning on greeting them all, but in a way I was responsible for adding the finishing touches to their night out.

It was my role to carve and create the chopsticks. Yes, every guest was given a handmade pair of chopsticks. For all pre-bookings, we even personalised the chopsticks with their names.

It was always assumed that it was my father who carved the chopsticks. No one knew it was actually me.

I know what you're thinking? Why on earth would we do that?

Well, I figured we needed a hook to attract our customers.

Each guest got to take away their chopsticks as a memento of their evening at the House of Wu. We were the only ones to ever offer this service. Others went down the fortune cookie route with the cheap and tacky messages. Where's the unique selling point in doing that? We only resorted to fortune cookies during Chinese New Year or the New Year, as we know it, and ensured that the messages were deep and meaningful.

I loved helping my parents and found the carving of chopsticks to be a very therapeutic and relaxing activity. It also required a lot of precision work, which I thoroughly enjoyed. Anything to keep my mind active made me happy.

When I first started school my parents gave me a personalised stationery set. Every item had my name printed on it and that's where I got my inspiration for the chopsticks.

At first, my father thought it was a crazy idea. But after I promoted it through social media, bookings increased by 300%. As a result, we had to take on more staff to cope with the demand, especially on weekends and during the holiday season. We even had travellers from far afield visiting just for the chopsticks. My father quickly came on board and even helped ensure that I had a regular supply of the best wood available, sourced directly from China. My father claimed that the wood was one of the hardest and toughest in the world and an excellent choice for making utensils.

He even suggested that we carved the names in mandarin, but that would have been way too challenging for me!

The menu was down to my parents and boasted a delightful selection of seafood dishes. If you were ever passing by, then I'd highly recommend the black cod and chips or perhaps the spicy chilli crab, served with fresh homemade bread rolls, perfect for dunking in the rich sauce. They were my fusion favourites. The black cod and chips might sound normal, but I assure you that there was an added twist to it with the special blend of spices that were used to season it. The cod would simply melt in your mouth.

Aside from carving chopsticks, I also helped with greeting the guests and occasionally I would serve at the tables.

My parents hard work ethos had rubbed off on me and I too wanted to succeed in all that I did.

I was always a devoted, loving daughter to whom her parents meant the world. My love and feelings were genuine and I was true to myself. If I didn't like something, I would say so. I could be very direct if I wanted to be.

The House of Wu was the foundation of their dreams and I was determined to ensure that it remained successful, whilst always helping to push through and break boundaries. A bit like my ever changing, fusion menu, that had been designed to cater for a younger crowd. It worked a treat, but I was always tinkering with it.

There was never a quiet night at the House of Wu, as the tables were usually full every night.

The House of Wu was homely and simple. There were no grand chandeliers hanging from the ceiling. Instead, there were tall red cylindrical lanterns. In Chinese culture, they were a symbol of booming life and a prosperous business, with the red colour symbolising good fortune and joy.

The walls were covered in mosaic style wallpaper, which was green and yellow in colour. Green was associated with health and prosperity whilst yellow was considered a prestigious colour to use.

When I questioned it, father always said that 'Yellow generates Yin and Yang', implying that it was the centre of everything. It was also the symbolic colour of the five legendary emperors of ancient China and was often used as the colour to decorate royal palaces. Well, the House of Wu was my parents' palace.

A few paintings and sepia photographs of Zhejiang were also hung on the walls. They were both personal and meaningful to my parents.

There were eight round wooden tables each able to seat eight people; only, the tables weren't numbered one to eight. When I questioned why, my father was always quick to remind me about tradition.

In Chinese tradition, certain numbers are believed by some to be auspicious or inauspicious. The number eight is associated with prosperity hence eight tables with eight seats whilst the number four is a strict no-no as it represents death.

My father ensured that certain traditions were respected and he felt that was a key ingredient in maintaining the integrity of the House of Wu as an authentic Chinese restaurant.

The tables were covered in a traditional Asian runner with a small jade tree as the centrepiece.

The décor entirely was down to my parents. I am still in the lukewarm camp as to whether it worked as a setting for a cosy warm restaurant. When you visit us, you'll understand what I mean. I was convinced that it was the food that made people return, time and time again and not the décor.

I'm not fussy. I'm just speaking my mind. We all have individual tastes. Whenever I questioned it, I was constantly reminded that it had a touch of Zhejiang in it and that it was important for one not to forget ones roots. What do I know? It's not as if I've ever been there.

Meet the boss, Mr Wu, or as I prefer to call him, 'dad'.

"Hello princess how was college?" asked dad.

"It was good. I really enjoyed it!" I replied rather excitedly.

"I did seem to attract a lot of attention from the guys as well as strange looks from the girls. Guess I'll have to be careful," I added.

"Remember all that we have taught you, about peace, tranquillity and self-respect," added dad.

"Yes father," I replied.

He was always 'father' when he was in a serious mood and 'dad' on those rare occasions that he let his guard down and was fun.

Father always taught me to be patient in all that I do and to use spoken word instead of veering towards violence. In fact it was something more like 'speak the truth, do not yield to anger'.

My father was an educated and well-read man. His beliefs were very much guided by the teachings of Confucius. My father had embedded me with the well-known principle 'What you do not want done to yourself, do not do to others'.

Despite always following this principle, I never once felt that the energy and effort that I put in on a daily basis was ever reciprocated, in anything I did in life, especially when it came to friendships.

Father also was a strong advocate for sincerity and the cultivation of knowledge. This probably explains why I can sound boring at times. Just like Confucius, he too felt that a sincere thought begins with knowledge. Therefore cultivating knowledge and sincerity was important for one's own sake; after all, the superior person loves learning for the sake of learning and righteousness for the sake of righteousness.

Have I confused or lost you?

Now I'm beginning to sound boring again and serious like my father, where's the fun in that?

What father was trying to say was that knowledge was a far more potent power than a makeup bag! The more you learnt about life, about cultures, about other people, the more you benefit as an individual and those around you also benefit.

What about my mother, I hear you ask?

Well, Mrs Wu, mum, was simply the most amazing mum you could ever ask for. She was the perfect wife, mother and a pillar of strength for both my father and I.

She was in charge of running the business on a day-to-day basis. She was meticulous when it came to paperwork and rules that needed to be adhered to.

She was also there to nurture and support me through all my troubles. I'm not saying that my father wasn't there, he always was. But motherly love is very special and endearing in its own unique way. I guess us girls need our girly times too, and it wasn't as though I was always getting myself into trouble.

She loved my father very much and the two were amazing together. My fathers eyes would light up and his face would glow at the sheer presence of my mother and vice versa. And if ever she was ill, it was almost like the end of the world for him.

My mother and I often started each morning with a Tai Chi session. She used it to embed the values of knowledge, sincerity and humility into me. My mother always said that whilst it was a martial art and provided skills for defence training, it was the health benefits that were more important. It would help me to improve my balance and enhance my psychological health.

I was an only child. I know how much it would've meant to my parents to have more children, but they never did. I don't know why they chose to have no more children. Had they been in China, then I could understand with the quota system they had in place at the time.

My father was an Ox, according to Chinese astrology that is. Ox people are hardworking and persistent; they can stick at a task longer and go at it harder than anybody. This was true of my father. He never knew when to stop and giving up was not an option for him.

I was always told never to cross Oxen, as they could be very impulsive when they are angry. But luckily, I never saw my father angry. Upset, yes, but not angry.

My parents lived a very simple, humble life. They had no enemies and no ill feelings towards anyone. They always preached happiness, sincerity and to love thy neighbour.

My parents gave me the freedom to develop into the person that I am today. There were no pressures from either of them and no rules to follow. Guidance, yes. Rules, no. They just wanted the best for me and wanted to ensure that I received the finest education possible.

Whilst their aspirations centred on the House of Wu, they wanted me to aim much higher.

Let's go back to my mother for a moment.

She was truly one of the most beautiful women you could ever meet, pious, loving, caring, loyal and incredibly stunning. When we were together, she was often mistaken for being my elder sister, as she didn't look her age. Never once did she raise her voice and she was ladylike in every manner.

They say that behind every successful man there stands a strong, wise and hardworking woman. This was very true about my parents.

My father had an ally, a soul mate and a rock that he could always rely on. Their bond was strong and grew stronger as each day passed by.

My father was head over heels in love with my mother from the first time that he set eyes on her. From that moment onwards he knew she was the one for him.

I questioned how and what that feeling was like, but his reply was always very formal, "The day you meet your soul mate, you will just know."

I loved my father. But he always had to portray that he was strong, tough and manly. I wish he had shown his softer side a little bit more.

Mother just said that it was a cultural thing. But then again, she always stood up for him, no matter what. Were men in China all like this? A closed book when it came to emotions? I wasn't sure.

Apparently, family elders didn't approve of my parents' marriage but through sheer determination and will power they made it work.

That was the strength of my parents bond. No matter what challenges they faced in life, they always found a way to overcome them. They firmly believed that true love coupled with a tight bond could overcome all hardship in life. It was always about channelling your energies in positive meaningful ways; the more negative energy that you had inside you, the more likely you were to be presented with roadblocks in the pathways of life.

Just hearing some of their stories about the hardship that they faced was an eye opener.

My mother always said that the hardship that my parents faced in life gave them the strength and direction in order for them to navigate their new world.

My mother was like an open book. She shared everything with me. That is, apart from her life back in China. My father was the same. That subject was unusually off limits.

I knew that my parents longed to go back and visit their home, but something always held them back. There were too many excuses that were used as to why this wasn't a good time or that wasn't a good time.

It was as though they had left behind unfinished business and never fully achieved closure prior to moving on.

They lived a life that was well-balanced ensuring harmony with western ways and some of the cultural traditions that they had become accustomed to.

Maybe I was being paranoid, but I always felt that perhaps they had some dark hidden secrets that they were protecting me from. Maybe that was the excitable child in me, living in hope that there might be some overwhelming mysterious past that they share!

Both of my parents were ambitious and hardworking and always set high standards. This was the blueprint for the Wu family and it was important for me to never deviate from these standards.

I also needed to fully understand and respect the family traditions and find a way to balance tradition with modern life.

My parents always said how proud and blessed they felt to have me in their lives. They said that the day I become a parent is when I will realise and fully understand why they always felt that way.

My parents had immense belief in me. At times I felt that it might be a huge weight for me to carry on my shoulders, but in many ways I was proud to be in this situation.

In fact, I was very proud and lucky to have them.

Aunt Daiyu is the only other family that I have in New Valliant City. She is the younger sister of my mother. I'm quite close to her although I don't see her much lately, as she travels a lot as part of her job.

Aunt Daiyu lives on the opposite side of the city. Personally, I don't think it's as nice and homely as where I live. It's currently undergoing a facelift and as a result, there are a lot of dormant and derelict properties nearby.

So, there you have the House of Wu and my family.

Home is Where the Shops Are

They say that home is where the heart is. My parents' home will always be Zhejiang, whilst this will be their adopted home. But for me, this will always be my home. That's a lot of homes to get your head around.

New Valliant City is a diverse, multi-ethnic and cosmopolitan city that has so much to offer, especially considering that it has a population of almost two million.

The city still has its fair share of grand historic architecture and listed buildings, but it's the growing number of iconic developments, which define the city's landscape today. This includes the Grand Central shopping complex, the new jewel located in the heart of the city. In fact, the whole city has been undergoing a major transformation over the last few years and there's more to come.

The centre is also home to a number of art galleries and museums, including the recently revamped science and history museum. Then there is Grand Central library, which houses every book you can possibly imagine.

The city is a strong advocate for learning with a number of colleges and two universities. The learning quarter is growing stronger year on year and that is good for the city.

There is a lot of industry present in the city thanks to its industrial past as well as a very strong emerging service sector. Unemployment is very low and the city is thriving in every aspect.

Come to think of it, maybe I'm beginning to understand why my parents chose to settle here. The city has so much to offer and there is so much more to come.

Away from the centre it has many cultural hubs, like the Chinese quarter, the Indian quarter, the Irish quarter and even a Spanish quarter.

Each cultural hub is distinctive when it comes to sights, sounds and smells. The hustle and bustle of the various communities paints a colourful picture and the aroma from the various food outlets is mouth-watering, each taking you back to the origins of the respective cultures. And then there are the many different spoken languages and dialects.

It is an old city with lots of embedded history and many untold stories.

With a well-connected public transport network, it makes it very easy to get around quickly without a car. The extensive road network means that you can get between most places easily but it isn't always quick thanks to the traffic. I don't know why I'm even telling you this, as I can't drive yet!

It's a friendly place to live and generally has low crime rates compared to the national average. Where we live, the crime rates are even lower. To top it off, there's a really vibrant community feel to this place and perhaps that's the main reason that my parents opted to stay here. Other areas might have neighbourhood watch schemes, but we have each other. It's very neighbourly and in the summer, there are plenty of barbecue parties taking place. In fact, people around here don't need an excuse for a get together.

Now I'm sounding like the local tourist board trying to sell the delights of my home city. Well that was what made this city so unique. You'll find an advocate and promoter in every one of its citizens.

My parents never said why or how they ended up here. They just did. One thing was for sure; the city provides so many opportunities for business and growth in every aspect. If the House of Wu was going to be a success, then this was the perfect city for it.

The House of Wu is located in a residential area, in amongst a small parade of shops alongside Franco's grocery store and Beryl's Cakes & Buns.

Franco's is a family run business that has been in the family for generations. Beryl's is a first generation family business. Beryl, the owner is very feisty and has high aspirations, just like my father. The parade of shops gives the area that extra special feel to it.

I'm a girly girl and for me, home is where the shops are. I spend most of my spare time at Grand Central, the shopping complex.

Grand Central is located in the centre of the city next to the old train station. It has over a hundred stores located within the same complex making it the perfect place for me. It isn't the only shopping complex in the city, but as it is in the centre, it is ideal.

The older parts of the centre are still undergoing changes and there's an even bigger shopping centre planned in the next few years. The sooner the better is what I say, especially if there's another few hundred shops planned.

A girl's got to shop, right? Well, I'm no exception. I'm always shopping, whether it's for a new outfit, shoes, boots, you name it. Yes, that's footwear in there twice. Get the feeling that I have my own footwear collection? I simply love shopping, whether that is window-shopping or actually spending my savings.

I enjoyed life's luxuries but under my parents guidance, I was always taught to live within my means.

Shopping aside, I have many other interests. I love learning about different cultures, ways of life, languages and history. I have what you would call, a thirst for knowledge. My home city provides the perfect base for me to quench this thirst.

Grand Central also provides the perfect hangout for a lot of the teenagers in the city. There's the bowling alley, an ice rink, cinemas, restaurants as well as numerous cafés. Oh, and have I mentioned dessert places? Yes, I love my desserts be it a chocolate cake or dairy ice cream although both compliment each other very nicely.

My home city is a city that never sleeps in which there is always something to do, especially if you have a lot of friends, which I did not have.

Friends

I somehow was never loud enough to be a part of the other girls circle of friends. Uptight and weird were just two of the tags I was given.

I'm a simple girl. Yes, I have exotic features, which can be attributed to my beautiful mother and the origins of my family, but I am my own individual person.

On occasions, I was actually told that I drew too much attention due to my looks. Can you believe that? At times, I felt that there was a racist undertone to the comments, but I had no way of proving them right.

My parents taught me to respect one another and to live a simple life. As a result, I was never vying to be the centre of attention. It was so not me.

In my younger days, I was often seen as a misfit as I was the only oriental looking pupil in class. Even the teachers singled me out on more than one occasion. I had a strong dislike for school for that very reason.

I often had a label attached to me. The one that I always found amusing was Miss One Hundred Percent! It was probably because I always gave my best efforts in all that I did and never shied away from hard work. A hard worker is the phrase that I would use. But I never got a hundred percent in an exam!

One person that truly knew me, or so I thought she did, was Maria.

Maria and I were very close right up to the last year of school, until her boyfriend allegedly took a liking to me for which I got the blame. We were like sisters and yet, overnight I became her public enemy number one. Nothing ever happened between her boyfriend and me.

I heard rumours circulating, which suggested that it wasn't her personal decision to end the friendship with me but one that was driven by her parents, or rather, her father. I had no way of validating whether this was true. She simply refused to discuss the topic with me. Why would her father accuse me of wanting to steal her boyfriend?

There were rumours that he was a very powerful businessman and not one to cross. As a result, I wasn't really keen on approaching him and asking him what I had allegedly done.

Nevertheless, the rumours never went away. Maybe it was a matter that later on in life would be resolved. Only time would tell.

I hear she too had enrolled in the same college as me, so who knows what destiny might bring. Would I forgive her? Yes, each and every time through sincerity and righteousness. My father once taught me that to forgive someone was the humblest of human traits yet the most rewarding in many aspects, after all, we are all human and humans are not perfect.

Boys, boys, boys! Yes, there were a lot of boys in my life. Mostly, obsessed with wanting to go out with me, although I did have my fair share of shall we say, 'anti-admirers'. That's all I'm saying!

I didn't once reciprocate with my feelings or actions. They even thought that I was more interested in girls as I was never interested in guys.

My parents had always guided me along the right path, always reassuring me that when the time was right, I would meet my prince charming and that time would be after my studies. They were very sure of that.

The reality was that nearly every single boy that I had crossed paths with left no footprint in my life, as they passed through. That's how I measured friendship.

Boys that came close were eventually overcome by temptation or peer pressures and wanted more than just friendship. You know what I'm referring to; it's the whole boyfriend-girlfriend thing.

Steve was one that fell into this category. We met when I was fifteen and by the time I turned sixteen, he felt that I was the one he wanted to spend the rest of his life with!

I was his first love and friendship alone wasn't an option for him.

He didn't ever understand why I had such a strong stance. It's not that I didn't like him. I mean after all, he was cute. But he was insecure and very possessive.

At the time, I was overawed that someone could feel so strongly about me. But I wasn't ready for a relationship of any sorts.

I'm not strange in any shape or form. I simply had strong views, morals and principles. My ambitions in life meant that I had no choice other than to behave in this manner. Although, when I had weak moments, my mother would usually be there to help guide me to follow the right path.

So now I have portrayed myself as a cold-hearted individual, which couldn't be further from the truth as I longed to be swept off my feet by my prince charming.

At the same time, I never had the environment in which I could be myself, let alone understand who I really was. At the age of sixteen, does anyone? I mean, I've heard the saying that life begins at twenty-one, or is it that life begins at forty?

Maybe college would finally provide me with an environment and platform for me to express who I really am. An environment in which people didn't play games with your emotions and one in which people acted grown-up and mature.

After all, like-minded, ambitious students craving to learn would surround me, wouldn't they?

College Life

College life was interesting. It was like an assorted box of chocolates; only there were more of the flavours that few of us liked. You know the type I mean, the ones with the runny centres or the coffee creams. Yuck!

I suspect that some thought that I was one of those flavours.

I liked to dress classically, elegant but simple. You'd often find me in pastels, pinks mainly, feminine colours. I liked my dresses but I wasn't averse to wearing jeans either. As for my taste in footwear, well, I did have a lot of shoes and a few pairs of black knee high boots. You know the ones I mean, the stretch type. And I'd finish it all off with a smart casual jacket. Simplicity was elegance in itself. I certainly wasn't the type to try and wear less in order to impress, unlike most of the girls in college. I mean, look at Jenny. Is that top even legal? And Sabrina, is that a bikini top? Why would you dress like that to college?

The only thing I would change is my hairstyle. Sometimes up, sometimes down. It definitely wasn't linked to my mood.

Anyway, it was Monday and I was on my way to the library. As I approached the entrance, I almost walked straight into Maria.

She was dressed in a black pin stripe dress with black and white shoes. It was her favoured classic look. My initial reaction was "Wow, nice outfit!" but I kept that to myself.

She was alone. We both stopped and looked at each other. Uncomfortable. That's how I'd describe it. That piercing quietness about a situation that makes all those who are present feel very awkward.

"Hi," I said.

Maria looked straight at me. It felt as though her eyes were about to pierce me.

"Wendy...Hi, how are you?" she replied. She was very quiet and surprised.

"Good, thanks. You?" I asked.

"Yeah, I'm good," she replied.

"I've err, got to head to class, I'm running late," she added, before heading off.

I kept looking at her as she hurried down the corridor. Then, she paused, looked back towards me and then away. I was sure that she wiped her eye as she headed out of sight.

Well, that was interesting, I thought to myself, a far cry from the last time that we met. That was the time when I tried to prove my innocence to her, but she just didn't want to know and directed all kinds of verbal abuse at me. It wasn't pleasant.

Maybe she had realised that I wasn't the cause of discord between us. I did miss her and our friendship but had learnt to live without her.

I was curious about behaviour and was always trying to work out what made people tick. Maybe that's what made me take up psychology.

I was a loner in many aspects.

I was happy and content as I watched other girls competing for the good-looking guys; and yes, I had witnessed a catfight or two.

I knew that when the time was right, my love would find me, by captivating my mind, body and soul in the process. I guess I too could be a woolly, fluffy, happy-go-lucky dreamer at times.

If only love had found its way to others. I'm referring to Julie Nash and Veronica Stiles. It wasn't long before I was introduced to them and it wasn't a pleasant first meeting in the cafeteria.

The college cafeteria was where students generally hung out in between class, so naturally I went there.

Double doors formed the entrance to the college cafeteria, through to a relatively large room containing lots of small tables, each able to seat four people. But in many cases, chairs were littered around the edges of tables, accommodating extended groups of students. There was a serving window to the kitchen that people got food and drinks from in the middle of the room and a large clock directly above the serving window.

There was the constant noise of students chatting away, some more vocal than others. If it weren't for the serving window, you wouldn't know it was a cafeteria. It felt more like a common room.

So, I was in the college cafeteria, sitting on my own, whilst enjoying a muffin and a hot chocolate. I was minding my own business and just happily getting on with my day.

Out of nowhere, Julie Nash appeared.

"Do you know whose table you're sitting at?" said Julie rather loudly.

I looked up and there she stood, tall, slim, proud and dressed like a goth, with what looked like black lipstick to match and hideous looking earrings.

"This table was free, so I sat down," I replied.

"It was free as it's a reserved table. It's our table and everyone knows that. You're new aren't you?" asked Julie.

Before I could respond, Veronica joined her. She was wearing a flowery dress and was definitely more feminine in appearance, despite being quite a large girl.

"Newbie girl sitting on our table, you know what that means Jules?" said Veronica.

As I was about to reply, Julia deliberately knocked over my hot chocolate. Luckily it wasn't boiling hot, as it spilled all over the table and slowly started to drip onto my clothes.

I looked around and instead of coming to my aide the cafeteria was beginning to empty very quickly.

Veronica just stood there laughing away at my expense.

I was covered in the chocolate drink and semi-numb at what had just happened. After a few seconds I stood up in an attempt to confront Julie.

"Why did you do that? What have I done to you?" I asked.

Julie just stared right at me, so much that I didn't see Veronica walk around me. Suddenly, I felt her grab my arms from behind.

"Don't you ever question us let alone challenge us. Don't you know who we are? Haven't we introduced ourselves enough?" said Veronica.

I was beginning to get the message loud and clear. I had just met some of the college bullies. I struggled and Veronica released me. I quickly grabbed my things and headed to the washroom.

I was upset at what had just happened, but more so as to the fact that no one came to help me. They all witnessed an injustice and just walked away. Is this what the world was coming to? Were people too afraid to stand up against wrongs?

I cleaned myself up in the washroom as best as I could and headed to my next class. It was a tough day at college, a real eye-opener.

I made sure I kept quiet about it, as it wasn't the kind of thing you discussed with anyone, even Andre didn't know.

Over the next few days, I witnessed Julie and Veronica bullying other pupils. The 'JV' partnership was one that was here to stay. This would not be my last encounter with them. That was something that I was very sure about. I wanted to make a complaint about them but as I was new, I needed to understand the workings of college a little more. After all, I didn't want to invite any more trouble.

The question I asked myself was just how many more bullies there were in college? Hopefully, no more.

You needed to be a quick learner at college and have a game plan. Julie and Veronica wanted to stamp their authority on the newbies whilst at the other end there were the endless popularity contests.

Lucinda Law was one of many Miss Populars, the new girl that everyone wanted to be friends with. Ironically, she was studying law and wanted to be a lawyer. Well, at least she had the perfect name.

She was intelligent, very pretty, tall and had curves in all the right places. Her appearance was immaculate and her dress sense was, well, stylish to say the least. Guys drooled at the sheer sight of her and girls craved to be like her, in every way, well, other girls, not me!

She had a close group of friends, ready to help with anything that needed doing, almost like her own personal aides. It was like something out of a college teen-movie, only this was real.

I hadn't had the privilege of meeting her, so didn't really know what she was like. I heard mixed views from others. Her close friends said she was simply amazing and the best friend you could have, whereas rumours were circulating that she was just a spoilt rich kid, always wanting to be at the centre of attention. I preferred to draw my own conclusions.

Her parents were rich, very rich. They were hoteliers and owned five star hotels in the city as well as a number of boutique properties in other cities. They were always in the news for one reason or another, although, I had never seen Lucinda on television.

Anyway, we shared a subject in college so it would surely be a matter of time before we met and became acquainted with one another.

Lucinda wasn't alone as there were others all wanting to be Miss Popular too. And then there were the guys too. Constantly flexing their muscles or ensuring their hair looked immaculate each time they walked past a mirror.

One thought sprung to my mind whenever I saw any of them preening in front of a mirror, "mirror mirror, who's the vainest of them all?"

One individual, who did leave a positive early impression on me, was Tara. She was simply stunning! She was tall, slim, very feminine, had the most gorgeous complexion and an incredible smile. She was well spoken, humble and came across as very sincere. In a word, she was beautiful and it takes a lot for me to say that.

We had only spoken the once, but I had seen her around in college.

I did have a tendency to just observe people and their behaviours. Think of it as research, after all, I was studying psychology.

Tara was a quiet girl who went about her own business in a private manner and was not an attention seeker. I liked her.

After all, I too was happy at just being myself, trying to keep a low profile.

Surprise, Surprise

It was Saturday, one of the busiest nights at the House of Wu and I was working front of the house. That meant that I was responsible for meeting, greeting and generally welcoming guests when they arrived, helping them to their table and talking them through the menu. I would also ensure that they were appointed a named waiter or waitress to look after them during their visit. It was hard work, but I enjoyed it as I loved meeting new people, even though at times I may come across as a loner.

Fridays and Saturdays were our longest days as we were open from 6pm through to 1am.

It was 7pm and the restaurant was full. It was buzzing and there were many a conversation taking place. The whole restaurant was filled with the delicate aromas of ginger and ginseng. My father always said how that evoked a sense of being right at home back in Zhejiang.

The House of Wu had its fair share of regular customers week in week out, yet today it was full of a lot of newcomers.

Cue another one of my crazy ideas, feedback cards.

I enjoyed receiving feedback from new customers, so that I could help to improve the House of Wu. In return for a completed card, I would hand out a ten per cent discount voucher for a meal at the House of Wu, thus encouraging a return visit.

A couple, whom I did not recognise, were just about to leave and I needed to take their payment. They handed over the bill together with a completed feedback card. It read:

'Noisy, crowded, filled with rich aromas, tasty food, and great service. Awesome!'

It always filled me with pride whenever I read positive comments like that and I knew my parents felt the same way too.

I processed the payment, placing the feedback card in the cash register and handed over a discount voucher. The couple were delighted and insisted on booking for the following weekend. I gladly obliged and completed their booking for them.

As they left, another group of customers arrived. It was usual for the weekend and it just never stopped from the minute we opened until it was closing time.

However, my eyes grew wide with excitement as I greeted the next pair, who once again, were newcomers to the House of Wu.

"Andre! Hi!" I said rather excitedly.

"Surprise, surprise!" responded Andre.

"We have a reservation, in the name of Duvall, for two, I believe," added Andre.

"Duvall…that's right, 8pm," I replied.

"Well, that would be us," smiled Andre.

"Duvall…Andre Duvall," I said rather inquisitively.

He never did tell me his surname or rather I never really questioned him.

Andre introduced me to his mother. First impression, she seemed very nice, I think.

I guided Andre and his mother to their table and talked them through the House of Wu menu and the day's specials.

I made a point of highlighting the dessert of the day, which was another one of my experiments, a lychee cheesecake. It was proving to be popular on the night.

"So, what brings you this way?" I asked.

"I heard that there was this great authentic Chinese restaurant hidden in this part of the city, so here I am," smiled Andre.

At that exact moment, my mother was walking by.

"Mother, may I introduce you to Andre, we attend the same college," I said.

"Sure, I'm Wendy's mother, delighted to meet you. And you must be Andre's mother, welcome to the House of Wu," replied mother.

"Thank you, delighted to be here and looking forward to the meal. Love the décor!" replied Andre's mother.

I decided to personally look after Andre during his visit and started by taking their orders.

A short while later father appeared from the kitchen to personally deliver Andre and his mother their meals.

I was surprised. My father only ever did that when it was close family or friends visiting. Clearly mother had already spoken to him.

"Err, Andre, this is my father," I said rather nervously.

Andre stood up.

"Mr Wu, it's a pleasure to meet you. Great restaurant you have here," replied Andre.

"The pleasure is all mine, young Andre, welcome. And to you, Mrs Duvall," said my father.

"A friend of my daughters is a friend of the House of Wu, please, enjoy your meal," added father, as he returned to the kitchen.

I smiled and left Andre and his mother to enjoy their meal, until it was time for dessert.

Andre called me over and placed an order for my lychee cheesecake. Was it out of politeness? I don't know. They certainly seemed to enjoy both the main course and dessert.

Once they had finished, it was time for the bill. My mother decided to take over.

Mother insisted that the meal was on the house as it was Andre's first visit to the House of Wu. But Andre's mother insisted on paying. After a friendly exchange of words and a bit of banter, they both agreed a compromise of a discounted bill.

I said my farewell to Andre and his mother and saw them out. I then returned to my duties.

After a while, I crossed paths with mother again.

"It was nice of your friend to visit," said Mother.

"Hmm hmm," I replied, and carried on working.

I was extremely proud of my parents with the way they welcomed Andre and his mother.

Over the coming weeks, Andre and I would meet on a daily basis in Bar Chocolato during any free sessions. I enjoyed spending time with him and getting to know him. Although, most of the time we would both be working on coursework or preparing for our next class.

Andre and his mother soon became regulars at the House of Wu too.

The Day Before

The day before my life changed was memorable for more than one reason.

It was a cold, dull and cloudy day. It had been raining heavily. For once, I wasn't organised and I had forgotten my umbrella. As a result, I was drenched on my way home from college. In fact, that's an understatement as I was wet through to my skin.

As I arrived home, I picked up the guest list for the House of Wu and headed upstairs, leaving a trail of water behind me. I got out of my wet clothes and took a hot shower. I knew I had to be fairly quick as I had another busy evening ahead of me.

I finished my shower, dried myself and got dressed. I quickly cleaned up the water trail that I had left. I always tried to help out with the housework, when I could.

This was followed by another evening of carving out chopsticks. Well, I never stop. I always like to be on the go and as my family were an integral part of who I was, I felt duly obliged to help them succeed in their dreams too. It was the Wu way and the only way that I knew.

If I wasn't making chopsticks, then I would be in the kitchen causing havoc with a wok!

Yes, you've guessed it, I would be found attempting to cook the next fusion special, usually with disastrous results to start with. Lately, I was hooked on desserts and was trying to create that perfect chocolate brownie cheesecake with an eastern twist.

So, there I was, helping out in the kitchen working away and just generally keeping busy. However, on this occasion, my mind was elsewhere. In fact it was focussed on Andre and deep in my thoughts was the friendship that we had started to develop.

I was happy to have a friend like him in my life. It seemed as though there were no games, no mood swings and definitely no hidden agendas. I was usually a very good judge of character and in a very short space of time I figured I had worked him out. His approach towards friendship mirrored mine and I was glad when he just turned up at the House of Wu, that very first time.

My parents were in the kitchen, taking a short break in between work.

Both of my parents were very observant. They knew me well and boasted how they could always read me like a book. I never doubted them once; after all, they never left my side when I was growing up.

"Wendy," said father.

I looked up towards him and feared that it might be the start of another one of his lessons in life. He had that look in his eye.

"You are only young once. Live your life, spend time with your friends and be happy. Follow your dreams and don't let anyone persuade you otherwise," he added.

I was taken aback. What brought this on all of a sudden, I thought to myself. My parents were usually the cautious type and strict too. Yet I was almost being given a free license to socialise more.

"Your friend Andre is a good choice. He makes you feel happy. He brings out the positive energy in you and that is a good sign. Always focus on creating positive energy around you. I believe you will know when you find the right partner," he went on to add.

Okay, so my father was giving Andre his blessings. That just felt very weird. It was the first time that he had ever agreed to me having a male friend. He always told me that Steve wasn't the one for me. Then again, we never did see eye-to-eye and he sure was right about that situation. But, he had only just met Andre. How could he make such a comment?

I looked towards my mother. She was smiling at me. Clearly my parents had discussed my friendship with Andre. Apart from his visit to the House of Wu on Saturday nights with his mother and the very little that I had discussed with my mother, they didn't know much about him. That's the thing about parents; each and every one has a detective inside them!

"Your father is right darling. We're both immensely proud of you. After all, you are our princess. In life you learn more when you make mistakes," said mother.

"Wherever you go, go with all your heart," added father, once again, quoting Confucius.

He always believed that if you are to do anything in life, no matter how big or small, always give it one hundred per cent and believe in yourself. Doubt and uncertainty in your actions would lead to hindrance in some form or another.

That made a lot of sense and I accepted this way of thinking. It wasn't always the case that I understood my fathers deep words.

Whenever I did anything in life, I always gave it my all, without fail. In doing so, it gave me deep satisfaction within my heart and I knew that I would never have any regrets in life. If it was meant to be, then it was meant to be.

I had never failed my parents and I guess it was their way of telling me that it was fine for me to make mistakes. They trusted me and had every faith in me. I guess I could understand the concept of learning from mistakes only I had yet to make one.

I was however a little confused. Why were my parents talking to me like this? Why today of all days? It just all seemed out of character.

We weren't a formal family and although my parents were very strict, they had their own style of explaining things to me.

Maybe I was being over analytical and perhaps I should have just been grateful for having such caring and understanding parents. Throughout my life they were there, supporting me, providing me with words of wisdom and guidance whenever I needed it. At times, my parents did tell me that I questioned things too much.

They were definitely perfect in every way.

Yet, something didn't feel quite right about this day. There was surely more to it…

The Darkest Day in My Life

It was a Thursday and I was due to spend some time with Andre after college. He was planning on taking me for a game of ten-pin bowling.

Andre simply could not believe that I had never been before. I guess it just never appealed to me. Maybe I always saw it as dull and boring.

But, in a strange way, I was actually looking forward to it. After all, my parents were very happy that for once I was actually not working or studying and was behaving like a college girl, whatever that was supposed to mean.

They liked Andre. My father felt that Andre was actually a positive influence on my life and a good friend to have. I didn't understand what father meant as he hadn't really done anything. Our friendship was still very young and developing slowly.

I remember the day well. I was wearing my favourite black stretch knee high boots, black jeans and a white stretch shirt. It was a smart casual look, perfect for college and casual enough for the evening.

Nothing much happened in college, I guess it was just a normal run of the mill day.

After college, I headed to Bar Chocolato to meet up with Andre. He messaged me earlier to say that he was running a little late. I ordered myself a small Bar Chocolato special and sat down. I decided to just watch the world go by whilst I waited for him.

It wasn't long before Andre arrived.

"Hey Wendy, sorry I'm late," said Andre.

"It's ok. Would you like a drink?" I asked.

"I'm good thanks. I'll have one at the bowling alley," replied Andre.

I finished my drink and we headed to the bowling alley. It was located in Grand Central shopping complex, which was a short bus ride away.

We arrived at the bowling alley in time for our pre-booked slot, paid for our game, changed our footwear and headed for our lane. The shoes were not what I would class as being stylish. Functional? Yes!

It was at that point that I first realised that the bowling alley actually felt like an extension of college. It was very busy and full of familiar faces from college, including the Miss Populars and the Gossip Queens. You know the ones that I am referring to, the ones who enjoyed talking about other people and were quite often the ones to start spreading rumours. Maybe now I knew why it was called Alley Cat Bowling. Not good!

I mean all the stories no doubt would begin about Andre and Wendy. You know how it is. Boy meets girl. Boy takes girl out to bowling. Boy must definitely be seeing girl, next they must definitely be planning on getting married!

I turned to Andre and told him how I felt.

"Andre, I'm feeling uncomfortable with all the looks that we're getting."

Andre looked around, paused and then replied.

"Don't worry. Let them think whatever they wish to think. Let's just enjoy our game of bowling and we'll worry about the consequences afterwards."

Andre was a mature, determined individual and not one afraid to challenge or take others on. Besides, he always had a naturally protective persona, which wasn't suffocating. I liked that. I could see why father liked us being friends.

After we ended our game of bowling, we decided to grab a burger. Not any burger, but a freshly cooked fish burger. Think of it as a research exercise for the House of Wu.

Before I forget, if you're wondering who won in bowling, well, Andre of course. I did well, but didn't want to end up beating him straightaway, did I?

And I have to admit it was more fun than I had perceived it to be. Maybe in my head I was thinking about bowls and not ten-pin bowling. I could try it again sometime. Then again, that would really get the whole of college talking.

As we walked to the burger bar, I felt a shiver shoot down my spine and for a few seconds felt a tingling sensation throughout my body. I felt unsteady on my feet. I put a hand out on the wall and steadied myself. Then, I was back to my usual self. It was almost like a precursor that something bad was about to happen, almost as though I was about to fall ill or something. Was I being over sensitive? I had a flash back to my childhood.

When I was young, I was involved in a small mishap or rather a small accident. I was trying to help my parents in the kitchen when somehow I managed to spill a very hot drink all over my arm causing a severe scald. I was taken to hospital and needed a skin graft. I was too young to remember the operation but I have a scar on my upper arm, which remains a painful reminder of what happened.

Since the accident, I became risk averse and the slightest sense of danger would be met with a tingling sensation throughout my body. I learnt to understand and live with this sensation and more importantly to trust my feelings.

One day when I was walking home from the nearby park, I decided to take a short cut through an alleyway.

Something didn't feel right but I ignored my instincts. As I entered the alleyway a dog appeared. I panicked and ran, only for the dog to give chase and eventually bite me.

Then there was the time at the supermarket when I was out food shopping with my mother. I was in an aisle containing tinned products. There I was admiring a rather tall pyramid display of tins when I had this strange feeling inside me. My mother called out to me and I started to walk in her direction. All of a sudden I heard a large bang. The pyramid display had collapsed behind me.

I tried not to think too much about the tingling sensation and put it down to nerves. After all, for once in my life, everything was going well and I felt happy, content and at peace with myself.

It was 5pm and I was still out. Usually I would be rushing to get back to help out my parents but today was my day off. My parents insisted that I took the day off.

"Milkshake and burger?" I thought to myself, only I had said it out aloud.

"Yes, would you like a milkshake to go with the gourmet fish burger? It's all about balance, remember," asked Andre.

I gazed up at the menu. Lots of choices, almost every fruit combination possible, I thought, until I spotted it. Damn! Double chocolate milkshake! You know I have a thing for chocolate and I guess so does Andre.

I smiled. Before I could respond, Andre spoke.

"Double chocolate milkshake, perhaps?"

"Mmm hmmm," I replied.

He was getting to know me very well.

We sat down and started chatting about life in general, recollecting how our first ever meeting went and how our friendship had developed.

It was nice. In fact, we didn't even notice when and who delivered our food, which was a far cry from our first meeting. The gourmet fish burger was so-so. But it provided me with food for thought. In fairness, I treated every so-so food experience as an inspiration for my fusion menu. I would often see it as a challenge to see if I could create something mouth-watering in its place.

As we chatted away, Andre soon realised that no matter what I did, or whom I did it with, my family was always going to be a big part of my life, as was food. This didn't seem to worry him much. In fact, he too had strong family values and said he simply understood family life. Then again, he never really spoke much about his family. He was always reluctant to do so. I figured when the time was right, he would open up.

Anyway, it was my turn to pay the bill. Andre was good in that manner. I settled the bill and we decided to head home.

We both lived in opposite directions. After saying our goodbyes, we headed our separate ways.

Unlike the day before, it wasn't raining and was actually a very warm day. Still, I wasn't taking any chances and made sure I had an umbrella with me. I could go on about the weather, as lately, no two days were the same. In fact, the weather usually formed a topic of conversation at least once a day.

A lot was on my mind, happy thoughts, happy positive thoughts. I was enjoying college life.

As I walked closer to home, I felt another shiver shoot down my spine and tingling sensations throughout my body. This time they felt stronger and lasted longer. I was struck by a sense of panic. Then I heard the sirens and saw flashing lights in the distance.

I noticed the pale blue sky turning dark very quickly. Something had happened. Something very bad had happened.

I carried on walking. With each step, I felt the tingling sensations getting stronger and stronger. As I got closer to home, it hit me. The sirens and flashing lights were coming from right outside the House of Wu. It was on Fire!

The happy thoughts were gone in a flash...

The Fire

The whole building was ablaze. Plumes of thick black smoke just billowed out across the sky and flames could be seen shooting from the windows and roof of the building.

For a moment, all I could hear was the loud thumping of my heart. I just froze to the spot whilst I took everything in.

I looked around and noticed firefighters carrying hoses everywhere. They were fighting what was quickly turning into a raging inferno. It was at that moment that I first noticed the strong acrid smell and the heat from the fire. It was unbearable.

There was a cordon around the parade of shops, yet crowds were still gathering, all gasping whilst watching the blaze. I heard someone mention that Beryl's and Franco's were also under threat from the fire and that firefighters were doing their utmost to save them too.

And then all of a sudden, there was an explosion followed by the sound of glass shattering. Things didn't look good for the House of Wu.

My breathing became very strained and that acted as a trigger for me to run towards my home oblivious of my surroundings. Suddenly two individuals in uniforms grabbed me. It was the police.

"Stop! Stop! You can't go any further!" shouted one of the police officers.

"That's my home! My parents are in there!" I screamed.

"Calm down, calm down," replied a police officer in a rather relaxed manner, as he took me to one side.

"My parents!" I shouted.

I became hysterical and started to scream. A policewoman approached me and put her arm around me. I knew something bad had happened.

"Come with me," she said, as she took me towards a police van. She opened the side door and I was helped to sit on the floor with my feet on the pavement.

I was visibly shaking and tears were flowing from my eyes.

"My parents are in there! Have you rescued them? Did they manage to get out in time?" I screamed.

"We're doing all we can to tackle the fire and rescue anybody that's trapped inside," replied the policewoman.

I had so many questions but at the same time just wanted to get sight of my parents.

"Can I start by taking your details?" asked the policewoman.

"I'm Wendy, Wendy Wu and that is my parents' restaurant and my home! What has happened?" I screamed. In fact, I became quite hysterical.

"It appears that there has been a fire. We were called out just over twenty minutes ago after receiving calls about a building catching fire. That's all I have for you at this moment. I don't know if there was anyone inside at the time," replied the policewoman.

I just stared at her.

"I'll need your help. Let's start with who you think might be in there?" asked the policewoman.

I froze and couldn't think straight. After about a minute, I responded.

"Err, my parents, I don't know who else, I don't know!" I said.

Without warning, I just stood up. The policewoman reacted fast, as she too stood up and put her hand on my shoulder.

I looked across and could see firefighters tackling the blaze. The House of Wu was fully engulfed in flames. I could see lots of people around but not my parents.

I started to call out for them.

"Mother! Father! Where are you?"

Tears started to flow uncontrollably again, as the realisation started to sink in. What if they were trapped inside?

At that precise moment, I heard the sound of a policeman's radio. There were people trapped inside the building. My legs began to buckle and I fell to my knees on the pavement.

There was water, steam and smoke everywhere. Small pockets of ash started to form on parked cars. It was a complete mess.

Suddenly, I saw a lot of movement. Firefighters, police officers and medics were rushing. A team of firefighters wearing breathing apparatus entered the House of Wu.

A few minutes later, they emerged whilst carrying two people from the burning building. They took them straight towards the waiting ambulances.

I could hear my heart pounding away in my ears. As the policewoman turned to speak to her colleague to get an update, I stood up and ran, through the police cordon and towards the ambulances.

I pushed through all the firefighters and saw two men on stretchers.

The two people they had taken into ambulances were not my parents.

I started to feel faint as my whole world started to cave in on me. It started getting dark very quickly and then I passed out. When I came around, I too was in an ambulance. There was an oxygen mask on me. I took a few deep breaths before pulling off the mask.

"My parents? Where are they? Are they going to be okay?" I asked.

The same policewoman emerged from a crowd looking rather glum.

"I'm sorry. The two people that we pulled out were not your parents," she replied.

"No, no, no, no, no!" I yelled.

"That can't be possible? Where are my parents?" I screamed.

"We're still searching for them," replied the policewoman.

I got up off my bed, ran out of the ambulance I was in and headed towards the neighbouring ambulances, to have a look inside. One of the men that firefighters had rescued was being attended to.

"My parents? Where are they?" I screamed, again.

The man that the medics were attending to sat up took off his mask and looked towards me. I reached forward and grabbed his filthy shirt. I asked him again about my parents but it was met with laughter, which started to become louder and louder. And then he just dropped backwards, as his head fell to the side. I noticed a strange looking tattoo on his neck. I was pulled to the side as additional medics attended to him. Commotion followed after which there was silence. He didn't make it.

The second of the two men was in a slightly better condition and he was swiftly taken to hospital.

Hope was fading for my parents.

"Is there anyone we can call on your behalf?" asked one of the police officers.

"My aunt, Daiyu," I replied, before sinking to the ground and bursting out hysterically into tears.

I truly felt that my life was over. After the recent positivity in my life, how could I be dealt such a damaging blow? My parents were trapped inside the House of Wu and I had to now fear the worst.

I wiped my tears and looked to the sky. I remember it well. It was dark with red-grey clouds and there was a full moon present. Smoke billowed across the sky.

My life had changed completely. I needed to dig deep.

As I rose to my feet, my legs gave way and I collapsed. It was as though someone had just turned out the lights on me.

Aunt Daiyu

Aunt Daiyu was the younger sibling of my mother and came across from China a year after my parents had moved.

She was married but was no longer with her husband. I don't really know what happened between them. It was one of those topics that we never discussed as a family. They say every family has its secrets and this was one of ours, or rather one of my parents.

I was very close to her. Not only was she my aunt but also someone that I turned towards at times of need and someone that I could confide in. She was like an elder sister.

As I opened my eyes, there she stood, tears flowing down her face.

I looked around and realised I was in hospital. I had collapsed at the scene of the fire and I had been brought here.

Luckily I mentioned Aunt Daiyu before I collapsed and the police were able to contact her using my mobile phone.

As Aunt Daiyu moved towards me, I sat up and leapt into her arms, embracing her very tightly. I started to cry. In fact, that was an understatement as I released all of the emotion inside me.

We held each other tightly knowing that somehow we had to remain strong for each other.

"Wendy, I...," said Aunt Daiyu, unable to complete her sentence.

"Have they found mum and dad?" I asked.

Aunt Daiyu looked away from me and slowly shook her head.

"I...I just...don't know," she replied.

At that split moment, I felt that there might be more to this tragedy than met the eye. It was almost as though

Aunt Daiyu was holding back on me. Her body language just didn't seem right. She didn't seem to want to make eye contact with me and seemed to be deep in thought.

I had no reason to doubt her, but sometimes in life you get that eerie feeling that something was not quite right and this was one of those occasions.

All of a sudden, two police officers, a male and a female walked in. We both turned towards them.

"Miss Wu, I'm sorry to have to inform you, but it seems that your parents didn't make it," said the female officer.

"It seems? What do you mean? Haven't you found them?" I asked.

"We have recovered two bodies but they have suffered extensive burns and are both unrecognisable. We believe that they are the bodies of your parents," replied the officer.

I started shaking my head.

"NO, NO, NO, NO! I will not accept that! You cannot assume that they were my parents," I said, rather emotionally.

The second officer stepped forward and spoke.

"One of the victims was wearing a necklace. Do you recognise this?"

The police officer passed me a clear plastic bag containing a burnt necklace.

As I held it in my hand, tears started to flow uncontrollably from my eyes and I dropped to my knees. The necklace consisted of three marble rings. It belonged to my grandmother and was one of my mother's favourite necklaces.

Aunt Daiyu moved towards me and put her arms around me.

"What about my father?" I said, whilst I sobbed.

"Firefighters found the charred remains of two people handcuffed to one another. The necklace was removed from one of the bodies," replied the male police officer.

There was a brief moment of silence.

"It appears that this was a robbery that may have gone bad," added the male police officer.

I had no response to that and there was no reaction from Aunt Daiyu either.

It was a fairly safe and friendly neighbourhood. Crime was almost non-existent, yet here I was being told that my parents were victims of a crime.

I looked lost. Numb with pain and the disbelief that something so callous and cold could happen to anyone let alone my parents. I was angry and my anger seemed to be building within me, but I was managing to supress it. Once again, I recalled fathers wise words from the teachings of Confucius, 'When anger rises, think of the consequences'.

It was almost as though he was my guardian angel, still watching over me despite the fact that he had left me.

"What about the two men that were rescued?" I asked.

"One of them did not make it. The second is in hospital and we intend to speak to him as soon as doctors grant us permission. He is currently under police guard so rest assured he will not be released him until we have spoken to him. I must point out that at this stage, he is not a suspect," replied the male police officer.

"Do you have any idea what may have caused the fire?" asked Aunt Daiyu.

"Fire investigators are still at the scene trying to assess what happened. As soon as we have more information, rest assured we will share this with you," replied the male police officer.

There was a knock on the door and a nurse walked in. She asked to speak to the male police officer and they both left the room.

Aunt Daiyu started to wipe my tears whilst holding me. As I looked up towards her, I noticed that her eyes were full of tears. The male police officer returned to the room and had a quiet word with his colleague.

"We have been given permission to speak with the survivor from the fire. He may be able to shed more light as to what happened. Please bear with us," said the male police officer as they both left the room rather hurriedly.

Again, I looked up towards my aunt.

"Aunt Daiyu, what am I going to do now? Where am I going to live? How am I going to cope?" I said rather tearfully.

Aunt Daiyu started to wipe my tears slowly.

"With me Wendy, with me. We have each other now and you will not be alone, I promise," replied Aunt Daiyu.

She was right. A huge chunk of our lives had just been taken away and it was down to the two of us to be there for each other, always.

From that moment onwards Aunt Daiyu had agreed to take me in and assumed full legal responsibility for me. I was truly blessed to have her in my life. Aunt Daiyu was special and unique in every way. I can't really explain why, but as you get to know her, you too will understand just why.

"Aunt Daiyu, can we leave now?" I asked.

"Let me see if I can get the nurse to discharge you," replied Aunt Daiyu, as she headed off to find the nurse.

As she left, I pulled myself together and wiped away my tears. I stood in front of the mirror and just stared at myself for a few minutes. I looked lost and broken.

A few minutes later, the door opened. It was Aunt Daiyu.

"Wendy, one of the duty doctors needs to reassess you before you can be discharged," said Aunt Daiyu, as she walked towards me and just held both of my hands.

We just stared at each other, both unable to muster a single word. Aunt Daiyu was trying to remain strong but each time I looked at her, I noticed her bottom lip quivering. I knew she too was hurting.

Suddenly, there was a knock on the door. It was the ward nurse and a duty doctor.

"Wendy, how are you feeling now?" said the doctor as he walked towards me.

The nurse proceeded to check my blood pressure whilst the doctor reviewed my notes.

"115 over 75 doctor," said the nurse.

"Excellent," replied the doctor.

"Wendy, I've read through your notes and I'm happy to discharge you. When you arrived, your blood pressure was very low. Shock can sometimes do this to you," added the doctor.

"Thank you," I said, quietly.

I breathed a sigh of relief as both Aunt Daiyu and I walked out together.

I noticed a number of police officers in the ward. It was at that moment that I realised I was in the secure unit within the hospital.

As we walked along a long corridor, I noticed a number of police officers standing outside a room. My heart started to race.

And then I noticed him, the survivor that was rescued from the House of Wu. He had very short black hair and a noticeable tattoo on his neck. I couldn't make out what it was of other than it was enclosed in a triangular shape.

He was talking to the police but it was his body language that didn't bode well with me. He was smirking and then laughing. My parents had lost their lives yet he was showing no remorse. Something didn't feel right at all.

We headed to Aunt Daiyu's, which from now on, would be home.

Survivor

A few days later, a police officer visited Aunt Daiyu's. I remember the day well.

"Wendy, Ms Daiyu. We have had a chance to speak to the survivor but I'm afraid he hasn't been able to assist with our enquiries in any shape or form," said the police officer.

"What do you mean, he hasn't been able to assist? He was rescued from the fire! He was in there!" I shouted.

"Please, calm down. I understand you're…" replied the police officer before I rudely interrupted him.

"Calm down? He was laughing in hospital! He showed no signs of remorse. Is that normal behaviour?" I asked.

"Wendy, we have no evidence to link him to the fire other than he was present. It's just a coincidence that he was there," replied the police officer.

"What was he doing in there?" I asked.

"He was a customer. He had a table booked," replied the police officer.

I paused for thought. Something just didn't add up.

And then it clicked.

"The House of Wu opened at seven on weekdays. What time did you receive the call about the fire?" I questioned.

The police officer just looked at me.

"I arrived at home at approximately six thirty and the House of Wu was engulfed in flames," I added.

The police officer had no answer to that.

"Both of the men had a strange tattoo on their necks. What was that about?" I asked.

"Wendy, it's a tattoo. It's not a crime to have a tattoo and that doesn't make him a criminal," replied the police officer.

"Look, I understand you're upset and hurt, but the harsh reality is that we do not have anything to go by at this stage," added the police officer.

I was beginning to get very upset. Here were the police telling me that the only survivor knew nothing, wasn't a suspect and that they had absolutely nothing to go by. They had no leads and were no closer to finding out what really happened.

"It looks as though it was an accident that caused the fire. We're still waiting for the forensic team to investigate," said the police officer.

"As for the survivor, we had to let him go. He was clearly in the wrong place at the wrong time," added the police officer.

I was livid.

"Wait a minute, you let the only lead walk free when his explanation clearly didn't add up! The House of Wu could not have been open for customers at the time of the fire," I asked.

The police officer looked a little startled. Surely the police had investigated the survivor's explanation before letting him just walk away. From the look on his face it didn't seem that way.

The anger inside me started to build and I couldn't believe what I had heard. I was just a college girl and I was beginning to question things more than the police.

"And then, how do you explain the reason for them being handcuffed together?" I shouted.

Remember, the bodies of my parents were found handcuffed together. Why wasn't the survivor cuffed? How did he survive and more importantly, how was he able to just walk free?

The police didn't seem to care. They knew best and they felt that they had no option but to let him go.

They had no answers to my questions, just excuses.

As he left, he advised us both that he would return in a few weeks once the forensic investigation had been completed.

I wasn't confident that it would be any better next time around. My faith in the justice system was fading very fast.

Back to College

It was a week after the fire and it was almost like the first day of college all over again. I woke up early and started to prepare myself for college. Aunt Daiyu was surprised to see me.

"Wendy, what are you doing awake so early?" asked Aunt Daiyu.

"My parents came here for a better life for me. They wanted me to have the best possible start to life and that meant a good education. I owe it to my parents to go to college," I replied.

"They taught you well. You are a Wu indeed, never one to shy away from adversity," said Aunt Daiyu.

Instead of allowing me to make my own way to college, Aunt Daiyu insisted on driving me. It meant a lot. I knew deep down that she was hurting too. Maybe she was just keeping herself together for my sake.

The journey itself was quiet and seemed to take ages. We couldn't muster a single word between us, although I did notice Aunt Daiyu looking at me a lot.

As we arrived at college I gave her a tight hug and a kiss on her cheek. I didn't want to let go of her and the tightness of her hug seemed to reciprocate my sentiments too.

I got out of her car and headed for college. As I entered the college grounds, I felt as though everyone's eyes were on me. I was clearly the talk of the college. A few of the girls approached me almost straight away. I didn't know who they were.

"Wendy, we're deeply sorry for your loss. If there's anything…" said one of the girls.

I nodded towards them and carried on walking.

I saw Andre in the distance, but he hadn't seen me. I quickly moved indoors and ran towards class. It was as though I had subconsciously decided to ignore him. I don't know why I did, but I just wasn't up to facing anyone. I felt upset, hurt and lost.

My head was all over the place. But at the same time, I was trying to remain strong. I could just hear my fathers wise words play in my head, time and time again.

'We should feel sorrow, but not sink under its oppression', once again quoting Confucius.

In class, my peers were surprised to see me. Not a single one approached me yet their eyes appeared sad. I knew I was going to be the subject of conversation today.

As class was about to start, there was a knock on the door. A female entered the room and spoke.

"Wendy, Miss Jones would like to see you in her office."

Miss Jones was the Head Teacher.

I collected my belongings and accompanied the female to the Head Teachers office, which seemed a long walk away.

As we arrived outside her office, the door opened. It was Miss Jones. My initial impression was that she was quite young to be the Head Teacher.

"Please, sit down," said Miss Jones as we entered her office.

She closed the door behind her and sat down.

I too sat down and just looked at Miss Jones. She was looking straight at me. There was an uncomfortable silence, which seemed to last a while. It was almost as though she had forgotten the reason as to why I was summoned to her office. And then she spoke.

"Wendy, let me start by passing on my condolences to you over your loss," she said.

I let out a huge sigh.

"Thank you, Miss..." I replied, in a soft tone.

"Are you sure that you're ready to be back in college?" asked Miss Jones.

I wasn't and I knew I wasn't. After all, who was I kidding? I was acting strong but deep inside, I was an emotional wreck.

"Yes...No...Yes..." I dithered.

Miss Jones could see that my head was all over the place.

"Wendy, if there is anything that I can do personally, I will. Think of me as a friend and not your Head Teacher," said Miss Jones.

I was surprised. The Head Teacher was offering to be my friend.

"I think you are an amazing individual to even contemplate coming into college so soon after the ordeal that you have endured. I don't know anyone who has demonstrated the courage that you are displaying here today," she added.

Miss Jones seemed sincere and I decided to take up her offer of friendship.

I was overcome with emotion and in the heat of the moment I decided to hug Miss Jones. She reciprocated only her hug was a lot tighter.

"Wendy, you should take leave for the rest of this week and come back after the funeral. You have just lost both of your parents. Take time to mourn your loss and remember, it's good to be tearful," said Miss Jones.

I looked at Miss Jones and remembered fathers wise words, 'Laugh and the world laughs with you. Cry and the world laughs at you'.

"The funeral is in two days. I am not sure how I will cope during that day and at the moment I prefer not to think about it. I just need to keep my mind occupied before then," I said softly.

Miss Jones stroked my hand.

"I understand. Whatever support you need, I am here for you," she said.

All of a sudden, the bell rang for change of class.

I did have another class, but instead I decided to take the cowardly way out and opted to head home.

The journey home was somewhat different. I didn't know what to do. I knew deep down that I would have to be strong and prepare for my parents' funeral.

The Funeral

I remember my father telling me about funerals and as always, he had a Confucian principle to quote, typically around devotion to your parents. I knew that it was my duty to help coordinate and prepare for the funerals.

Aunt Daiyu and I had consulted the Chinese Almanac to determine the best date for the funeral ceremony. Aunt Daiyu also explained what my parents final wishes were. It wasn't something that my parents and I ever discussed; after all, they were still in their prime. Who could ever envisage that they would be taken away from me so early in life?

Apart from Aunt Daiyu, we never really had any family here. Yet, we had sent out white paper invitations to their close friends and acquaintances. Aunt Daiyu had their details. I never did ask why.

Aunt Daiyu started to receive replies from the invites that were sent out requesting information about the wake. We decided to keep it short and just for one day and night, as per my parents' wishes.

The day before the funeral, Aunt Daiyu and I headed to the local temple, where the coffins containing my parents' bodies had been sent.

On arrival, we placed white candles around the coffins, lit them and just sat quietly in wait, taking a personal moment to reflect on their lives. A few close friends stopped by for a short while too, each one bringing some white flowers and a white envelope.

The envelopes contained money that was meant to help Aunt Daiyu and I pay for the funeral.

Aunt Daiyu and I had decided that we would keep an overnight vigil. Emotionally and spiritually we both felt we needed to do it.

Throughout the night, I could hear my fathers words of wisdom, echoing the thoughts of Confucius 'Death and life have their determined appointments; riches and honours depend upon heaven'.

He always said that if you lead a good life, and make good of yourself to other people in your lifetime, you don't need riches in your life. When you get to heaven that's when you're rewarded for your work, and your honour is being in heaven, living from the riches you created for yourself in this life.

It felt as though this was a farewell message from my father, his way of communicating with me and telling me that they are both resting peacefully in heaven looking down on me.

As morning approached, we headed home to prepare for the funeral. We were both braced for a rollercoaster of emotions.

My parents had wanted a simple send off and that meant two simple white wreaths, mother and father, and nothing else. Simplicity, remember. I found that very difficult to adhere to, but I just had to respect their wishes.

It was a warm and sunny day. In fact, it was the warmest day in weeks. The turnout for the funeral was amazing. There were over a hundred mourners present, whereas I guess I was expecting maybe a handful.

Aunt Daiyu and I were both dressed in black. We too kept things simple, whilst acting as a pillar of strength for each other. Not a single tear was shed by either of us from the time we arrived home to the time we got ready for the funeral and we managed to keep strong during the ceremony too.

Remember what father believed in, his reward for all he did in this life was a place in heaven along with my mother.

The ceremony was simple. I gave the eulogy for both of my parents. It was both difficult and emotional, but it was my way of honouring and acknowledging the amazing individuals that they were. They would have been extremely proud of me.

A short prayer followed the eulogy, after which it was time for the burial.

I was surprised that Aunt Daiyu didn't say a few words, but for some reason, I never questioned her.

The burial itself was filled with pain and a hurt that I will never forget. Seeing caskets containing the bodies of both of your parents being lowered into the ground, with the realisation that they never will be returning was a chilling and harrowing experience.

The burial felt like it took an eternity yet in reality it was over in minutes. The silence that surrounded it was deafening. It was very eerie and surreal.

Aunt Daiyu gripped my hand tightly sending a signal of support and strength to me. I let out a deep sigh followed by another. Tears flowed down my face during the burial, endless tears.

Once it was over, Aunt Daiyu wiped my tears and kissed me on my forehead.

As we turned to leave, an elderly Chinese gentleman approached us. He was well groomed and had a smart appearance. There were two tall men, with muscular builds, both wearing slick black suits and sunglasses, walking behind him. I could see they were both wearing earpieces with cables running under their collars.

Aunt Daiyu put her arm around me and gripped me tightly.

"I am deeply sorry for your loss," said the elderly gentleman as he lowered his head towards us both.

"Young lady, your father was a great man, full of principles and righteousness. Your mother too was a truly pious woman, always standing strong beside her husband. They will be missed," he added.

"Thank you," I replied in a soft voice that was about to break.

Aunt Daiyu's grip on me became tighter. Who was this gentleman? I noticed a tattoo on his neck, which looked like a dragon enclosed within a triangular symbol. The two suited men also had the tattoo. I had seen this before, but could not recall where.

It was strange. As he turned towards Aunt Daiyu, it almost looked like he smiled. Perhaps I was imagining things.

I watched him as he walked away and noticed the car or rather the convoy of cars that he had travelled in, clearly a sign of how important this person was. I turned to Aunt Daiyu.

"Who was that?" I asked.

"I don't know. An old acquaintance of your father no doubt," she replied.

Her voice wasn't convincing and neither was her body language, but, before I was able to probe her any further, I felt a tap on my shoulder. I turned around. It was Andre.

I had noticed him during the ceremony, as well as others from my college, but I tried not to make eye contact with any of them.

"I'm sorry for your loss," said Andre.

Tears began to flow and I was unable to contain myself. Andre's mother was present too and she reached out and hugged me, offering words of comfort.

"Thank you for coming," I replied.

Andre wasn't like the other guys I had met. He was always incredibly polite and sounded like a grown up. Being there with his mother meant a lot.

He wasn't alone. A number of students from my college were also present, including people whom I had never spoken to. They had attended the funeral as a show of support.

It was a very moving, touching sight.

"Thank you," I said, whilst wiping away my tears.

I realised that I wasn't alone anymore. It felt as though my peers had accepted me and warmed to me. Miss Jones was present too and she remained true to her words.

"Hello Wendy and you must be Aunt Daiyu. Please accept my condolences for the immense loss that you have both suffered. My words simply can't describe the emptiness, sadness and sorrow that I feel," she said.

"Thank you," replied Aunt Daiyu.

I was motionless at this moment.

"I'm Wendy's Head Teacher, but think of me as a friend. I can't imagine just how difficult it must be for you both. If there's ever anything that you need, please, call me," said Miss Jones, as she handed over a business card to my aunt.

As everyone slowly started to disperse, Lucinda Law appeared. She was the rich kid from college remember?

"Wendy, I am very sorry for your loss. Please accept my deepest, sincerest condolences. One can only imagine the magnitude of your loss and the pain you are experiencing," said Lucinda.

I was taken back. We had never spoken in college, and yet here she was at my parents' funeral. More importantly, she was well spoken, eloquent and seemed very kind.

"Thank you, Lucinda. Thank you for your kind words," I replied.

"Wendy, my family own several hotels in this city. If you need accommodation, whether it's for a day, month, year, as long as you need, I would be happy to help you," said Lucinda.

I didn't know how to react. Here was the supposedly rich kid that was always after attention, acting very humbly and honourably.

"I respect and admire you for the way you have handled yourself. I know we haven't met, but I'd like us to be friends," added Lucinda.

"Thank you, Lucinda," I replied in a soft voice.

Lucinda moved closer with her arms open and I took little time in embracing her with a warm hug.

"Keep strong," whispered Lucinda.

As Lucinda left, I reflected on the sad day that was my parents' funeral, the day that I said my farewell to both of them, a painful experience that I will never forget.

The whole day passed quickly. My parents had a simple send off with the sincerity of genuine mourners. It's how they would have wanted it to be. Aunt Daiyu was at hand to ensure their final wishes were respected and that was important to us both.

Apart from the endless tears during the burial, I somehow managed to keep it together.

Maybe it would have been better for me to just release the emotion that I had trapped inside me, but I knew that my parents would have disapproved of my behaviour.

As for the elderly Chinese gentleman, doubt remained in my mind and in my heart that there was more to him and his kind words, after I witnessed how Aunt Daiyu reacted, and that tattoo just would not go away. I was trying to remember where I had seen it, but my memory for once was not at its best. For today, I somehow needed to let go.

Tomorrow would be the start of a new day and a new chapter in my life.

Life After…

As the days passed by, I tried to come to terms with life after my parents. I kept thinking that each day would get easier and easier. Yet the reality of it was that each day I was supressing my anger more and more.

I was back in college and trying to just live a normal life, whatever that meant.

For the first time in my life, everyone was being nice to me, even the girls. The guys weren't harassing me either and in fact, they were genuinely being nice towards me. Yet, it took the loss of my parents for this to happen. Life could be very cruel when it wanted to be.

Still, at least I had a genuine friend in Andre.

He was there for me every single day. Often he would wait for me at the end of the day and accompany me home to my aunts, even though at times I would hardly speak. He hadn't changed at all. My parents were right about him too.

As for Lucinda, deep down, although we had only met briefly, I felt that we would somehow become closer.

As the days passed by, Lucinda and I made a concerted effort in acknowledging each other during law class. The respect for one another was mutual and I guess she knew that once my wounds had healed, we could get to know each other a lot better.

Tara also acknowledged me but we hadn't really spoken. I guess I never once felt like having a social life. It was the same routine, college and then home to Aunt Daiyu.

Andre knew I had been through a life-changing ordeal and could only begin to imagine how I felt. Yet this didn't seem to bother me. It was almost as though I didn't care.

Emotionally I was struggling to come to terms with my loss. My parents never had any enemies and always strived to do well. So why were they targeted?

My evenings were the same. After supper, I would lock myself away in my room. I tried to pretend nothing had happened but it was difficult. Part of me didn't want to move on.

I knew I needed to, as for a start I didn't have anything left. Everything I owned, including all of my childhood belongings had been lost in the fire.

Each night, I would continue to make chopsticks for the House of Wu that was no more. It was therapeutic and in some ways keeping me in touch with my parents. Maybe a part of me didn't want to let go.

Then again, I questioned why I did it, as it would always upset me that I was unable to personalise them. Maybe one day I could resurrect the House of Wu and make my parents truly proud. In fairness, I had not given the future much thought lately. I was taking each day as it came, step by step.

It was Sunday evening and I was in my room, busy carving chopsticks. Aunt Daiyu kept a supply of wood at her place. I never asked her why. It was just like the last ten evenings, although most evenings I would spend the time working on the same pair of chopsticks.

With each evening that passed by, with each chopstick that I carved, I could feel the hurt and pain turn towards anger that was getting deeper and deeper.

There were too many unanswered questions.

Why were my parents targeted? Why were they tied up? Why was the House of Wu set on fire? Who was the Chinese gentleman with the two suited men? Were they his bodyguards? If so, why did he need bodyguards? Did Aunt Daiyu know more than she was letting on? If so, why was she behaving in this manner?

With each question I asked myself, the anger inside me grew and grew. My life had been taken over by so many unanswered questions. I knew there was someone out there, more than just one person, who knew the truth behind my parents' murder. But it was being kept from me. No matter how hard I tried, I could not get the answers that I sought.

Suddenly, I felt the urge to release this suppressed anger.

I turned the chopstick that I was carving in my hand and threw it across the room. There was a dull sounding twang.

I looked up across the room and caught my breath.

The chopstick had become embedded in the door of my wardrobe. I was amazed and couldn't believe what was before my eyes. The very chopstick that I had carved out and then threw at the wardrobe was impaled in the wardrobe like it was a throwing knife or a dart.

I don't really know why I did it, but I decided to pick up another chopstick and threw that too.

Again the same thing happened. Adrenalin began to flow through me. I reached for more chopsticks and I threw these at the wardrobe, making a vertical line.

With each throw, I felt a huge sense of euphoria.

I was not the violent type. My parents taught me well. I remember father, often reminding me that 'what you do not want done to yourself, do not do to others'.

This applied to speech as well as all things physical.

I was taught to be very ladylike, from my posture to my dress sense, my spoken word to my respect for all those around me. I believed that elegance and simplicity were synonymous with each other.

Yet, here I was, an angry girl. Hate had started to cultivate inside me and I was in need of answers, answers that were evading me.

I got up and removed each chopstick from the wardrobe. I examined each indentation carefully. They were identical in depth. Wow! That was impressive. Did I really do that?

One of the chopsticks had strayed and hit a pair of my leggings that I had thrown on top of the wardrobe. They were hanging down over the front of the door.

I tried to remove the leggings without damaging them further but was struggling. The sharp end of the chopstick was impaled into my wardrobe, having pierced through my leggings. I couldn't just pull the leggings over the chopsticks, as the other end of the chopstick was thicker, making it an ideal area for engraving the names of guests. They weren't ordinary chopsticks.

I tried to remove the chopstick by force. In the process, I managed to rip my leggings. I didn't realise how deep the chopsticks had been impaled in the wardrobe.

My head was all over the place. I started crying and my body started to shake. It was almost as though I was no longer in control of my own actions.

I put the chopsticks into a bag, put it into my wardrobe under my clothes and then got changed for bed. Often now I didn't even brush my teeth or wash before bed. Tonight was no different, I simply cried myself to sleep.

I don't remember much about my sleep that night. But, I did wake up feeling relaxed and more at peace with myself than I had done since the fire. I took a quick shower and then had breakfast for the first time in almost a month.

After breakfast, I picked out a black dress to wear from my wardrobe, together with a black jacket and black stretch knee high boots. It was always a safe bet, as I could never predict what the weather would be like. Some days we could experience all four seasons in one go. I tried to guess what it would be like each morning and would change the dress to a warmer one if it felt too cold.

I closed the wardrobe door and saw the chopstick indentations.

I panicked. What if Aunt Daiyu entered my room whilst I was away? How would I explain it to her?

Without hesitation I removed a poster from the wall and stuck it onto the door of my wardrobe ensuring that it covered the indentations. I then headed to college.

It felt like my first day at college all over again, only, I felt different.

For the past few weeks, I would meet up with Andre first thing and we'd start the day with a chat over a Bar Chocolato special, but not today. Instead, I headed straight for class.

I felt coldness inside of me. I knew that Andre was a good guy and would be looking for me. But today, it was all about me.

Today, I felt restless, agitated and on edge.

I kept thinking about the previous night, my actions and my wardrobe.

In class I may have been present in body, but my mind was elsewhere. My peers attributed it to the shock of the ordeal that I had been through. I would have good days and bad days. Perhaps I could put today down as a bad day.

I heard some of the comments that were being made. I was incredibly brave and strong to turn up to college a few days after losing my parents yet now I was being told that it was all an act and I was out for sympathy.

I felt relieved. Gosh, the thought of being Miss Popular was nerve wrecking. I was better equipped to deal with being the girl that didn't exist.

It was rumoured that Julie and Veronica, the bullies from the cafeteria were responsible for expressing this view. And let's face it no one was likely to speak out against them.

Not once did I think about Andre throughout the whole day. Moreover, I somehow managed to avoid him without even trying.

In fact, I wasn't even sure if he was in college today. For once, I didn't care.

The Police

It was a very windy day and leaves were being blown everywhere. My hair too was being blown all over the place and there was just this strange feeling to my journey home. I can't explain it.

It was almost five weeks after the fire and I was just arriving home from college, when I noticed a police car outside.

I rushed to open the door and ran inside. Two police officers were already speaking to Aunt Daiyu.

"What has happened? Have you found them?" I asked rather excitedly.

I was studying law at college. I'm sure that I mentioned that. I was a firm believer in the justice system and had full confidence that the police would apprehend the perpetrators of the crime that had been committed against my parents.

"Miss Wu, we're doing everything we can to find out who committed the crime in order to get some answers as to why," said the female officer.

"Surely you must know by now, or have some firm leads, it's been over a month!" I said.

"Miss Wu, the truth is that we believe that your parents were victims of a robbery that did not go according to plan," said the male officer. From his demeanour and the stripes on his collar, it was clear that he was the more senior officer present.

Déjà vu, I thought to myself. They weren't much help during their previous visit either.

"They were tied up using handcuffs, in their own home which was then set on fire!" I said.

"Do you have results from the forensic investigation?" I added.

"Yes. It appears that accelerant may have been used," replied the male officer, before I interrupted.

"Accelerant? That means that the fire was clearly deliberate and my parents were murdered!" I replied.

"At this stage, we don't know. We believe that it started in the kitchen and that a cooker had been left on. It may have been a gas leak," replied the senior police officer.

"Then how do you explain them being tied up? It seems clear that it was all pre-planned!" I shouted.

The police simply shrugged their shoulders and didn't seem at all moved. I was stunned. I was struggling to comprehend their reasoning into any of this. The anger began to grow inside me and my faith in the criminal justice system was being sucked out of me.

"The truth is, a crime is committed every few minutes in this city, but most of it remains unreported. Seventy per cent of crimes such as robberies remain unsolved and the average time it takes to resolve a case is six months," he added.

"My parents were murdered! This was not just about a robbery!" I yelled.

"Please calm down. We're not saying that we will not resolve this case. But we have to be realistic. We have no motive, no witnesses, no evidence, we have nothing to go by," said the female officer.

"The survivor that walked free? Let me guess, you haven't been able to track him down again to re-question him?" I asked.

"He was a witness and was present when my parents were left in a burning building. He must have seen those responsible!" I added.

The anger inside me was growing with each comment and response from the police. I was flabbergasted. It's a miracle that they manage to solve thirty per cent of serious crimes, I thought to myself.

"We have already spoken to your aunt, but perhaps you can help? Do you know of any reason anyone would target your parents?" asked the senior officer.

I could not believe my ears. Now I was being asked if I knew why anyone would target my parents. They had always taught me about the virtues of peace and to never upset or offend anyone. I told the police. To my knowledge they didn't have any enemies. I could not comprehend why anyone would deliberately target them.

They took my statement and left, both leaving behind their business cards asking me to contact them in the event I find out anything useful or remember something important that I had failed to tell them about.

It felt like they wanted me to investigate the reasons as to why someone targeted my parents, murdered them and to let them know so that they could apprehend them and ensure justice might then be served?

The anger inside me had reached boiling point. My faith in the criminal justice system was lost. It had been shattered over the last few weeks, with each meeting with the police and investigating officers. Now I understood from the other side as to why people sometimes took the law into their own hands.

At college, I was being taught about how it was always wrong for a victim to take the law into their own hands, yet at first hand, in a matter of minutes, I had understood with ease as to why someone would cross that barrier.

In many ways, I could understand why victims felt that the law was no longer a deterrent for criminals and that even when caught, criminals would simply laugh in the face of the law. The police officers that visited me seemed to lack energy and drive and the desire to investigate.

I had heard about this, but never once experienced it. It hit home hard. Something needed to change. Something needed to be done about this injustice.

Help!

That evening, I felt very agitated and on edge. It was so unlike me, yet no matter what I tried, I could not change those feelings. I had even tried meditation, but that too didn't seem to help.

In addition to this, the anger inside me had reached boiling point and I was ready to overflow. I wanted to scream and shout, but I could not as Aunt Daiyu was asleep in the room next door.

I picked up my bag of chopsticks and one by one hurled them towards my wardrobe. The speed and accuracy with which I was throwing them was surprising. I felt empowered. I was energised and experienced a huge release of energy. I hadn't realised how sharp I had made the chopsticks that they could be used like a throwing knife or dart.

Suddenly, I felt that strange feeling of a shiver shoot down my spine coupled with a tingling sensation. These tingling sensations were beginning to become too regular for my liking. What were they signifying? Why was I getting them?

I walked over to my wardrobe and gazed at the chopsticks. In the background, I could hear the patter of raindrops. Great, I thought. It's raining. I pulled the chopsticks out of the wardrobe door and put them back into the bag.

Suddenly, I heard a scream. It was coming from outside. Probably someone playing games, I thought to myself.

A few seconds later, I heard a cry for help, "HELP! HELP ME!!"

I looked out of my window, but couldn't see anything.

My instincts took over. I knew Aunt Daiyu was fast asleep, so I grabbed my jacket, bag of chopsticks and quietly headed out to investigate.

It was a cold and dark night as one of the street lamps was out. I stopped and paused for breath. It was quiet again. Did I imagine the screams? Maybe it was teenagers just playing?

It had stopped raining, which helped as I could now try to figure out whether the screams were real or teenagers just playing.

A sense of fear struck me, as I was out alone, late at night. It was unlike me. I always played it safe. I turned around and decided to head back home. Suddenly, I heard the scream and cry for help again.

"HELP! HELP ME!!"

It came from the alleyway across the road. It was just a gap between two old office buildings that were now derelict and due to be demolished. It appeared cold and very uninviting. No one used the alleyway during the day, let alone dare venture into it during the night.

I started walking quickly towards it. I could feel and hear my heartbeat accelerating rapidly. My breathing had also changed and become quite heavy. As I arrived at the entrance to the alleyway, I sensed a strong smell. I didn't want to think what it was.

I noticed two guys and what looked like a girl. They were in the midst of attacking her, having taken off her jacket. She was doing her utmost to wriggle free. The attackers noticed me and looked straight at me.

"Hello there, come to party, have we?" said one of the attackers sarcastically.

I momentarily froze.

"Help me! Please help me!" cried the girl.

"Let her go," I said in a voice that was clearly trembling with fear.

One of the attackers let go of the girl and started to walk towards me.

"And what are you going to do about it? You'll have to join us now. Three's a crowd but a foursome is very wholesome," he sneered. He then broke into hysterical laughter.

"Run and get help, please!" shouted the victim of the attack.

I was in two minds. Do I leave and get help hoping that it would arrive in time to help the girl, or do I try and help her myself.

It was one of those moments in life when impulse simply took over and I just went with the flow, not even worrying about the potential consequences.

I reached for my bag and took out the chopsticks. My hands were trembling with fear. Somehow I needed to keep it together. I needed to be strong.

"Ha! Ha! Ha! Going to break my bones with sticks are we?" said one of the attackers as he stopped, leaned on a waste container and burst into laughter.

"Sticks and stones won't break my bones, but I'm going to hurt you real bad!" he yelled.

I didn't think.

I immediately threw a few chopsticks towards him with the speed and accuracy that I had practiced with in my room. They were aimed straight at him and each one met him with precision and accuracy.

The speed and trajectory of the chopsticks had a direct impact as he was pinned through his clothes to the waste container that he was stood in front of. He was unable to move.

I started walking towards the second attacker. My confidence was building.

"Let her go, now!" I shouted.

Immediately he let go of the girl by pushing her to the floor and started to turn towards me.

"I'm going to teach you a lesson, girlfriend! You're in the wrong place at the wrong time!" he screamed.

His accomplice, who was pinned up against the waste container shouted.

"James, help me get loose. I suggest we teach her a lesson she'll never forget."

I threw a chopstick towards the second of the attackers.

To my amazement, he caught it with his bare hands and as a sign of his strength he broke it in half.

"Is that all you've got?" he laughed, as he started charging towards me at speed.

I reached into my bag and pulled out more chopsticks.

This time, I took a handful and threw them with more purpose. On this occasion, he simply had no answer for them and I managed to pin him to the fence.

"Go! Get out of here and go home!" I shouted across to the girl.

She picked up her bag and jacket off the floor and quickly walked past me, without uttering a single word, not even a thank you, and not even making eye contact.

Both attackers were screaming and shouting towards me, telling me how they were going to hurt me, when they broke free. This then extended to a level of abuse that was sickening to hear. They started wriggling in order to break free.

Without giving it anymore thought, I turned around and took off home.

My heart was pounding and I was in a state of shock. I couldn't believe what I had just done. My actions went against everything that I had ever been taught.

I arrived home and quietly made my way to my room. I locked the door to my bedroom and just collapsed in a heap next to it.

I was shaking and felt exhausted as the adrenalin began to wear off. What had just happened? I started to think of the consequences had things not worked out. I too could have ended up like my parents, and then what?

I started to feel faint. I closed my eyes and drifted away for the night.

The Day That Was…

The following day, I opened my eyes and looked around, hoping that the previous night's events were just a bad dream.

Sadly, I was wrong.

I was lying on the floor, still wearing my jacket and boots. My clothes felt a little damp as it had been raining the previous night. In front of me, was my bag containing a few remaining chopsticks. Some were spread on the floor.

I gently got myself up and looked in the mirror. As I stood tall, I sensed a feeling of pride.

For the first time since I lost my parents I felt empowered and happy.

Visions of my parents screaming for help flashed by me only on that occasion there was no one to rescue them.

What happened last night? Was that destiny?

I thought about the last few weeks and recalled how I felt on the night of the fire and last night. There was something in common that happened on both nights, the shiver shooting down my spine and tingling sensations. It was almost as though I was developing a sixth sense only it was related to something bad that was about to happen.

Clearly, I was being over sensitive and over analysing everything. I laughed it off. Sixth sense? I must be losing it, I thought to myself.

I took off my clothes, grabbed a towel and headed for the shower.

The feeling of hot water running off the top of my head and down my back was refreshing. The steam from the hot water filled the shower and it felt invigorating. I closed my eyes and just stood there for a few minutes whilst gathering my thoughts.

What if someone had seen me? What if the attackers or the victim were able to identify me? Then what? I could be in serious trouble, I thought to myself, for a split second.

Under normal circumstances, I would panic and fear would overcome me. Yet, my immediate reaction was a simple smile.

I finished showering and dried myself. I decided to quickly dry and straighten my hair before getting dressed. I then headed downstairs for some breakfast.

I was alone as Aunt Daiyu was still asleep. I treated myself to two slices of toast, a banana and some cereal along with a glass of freshly squeezed orange juice. It was the biggest breakfast that I had eaten in weeks. I gathered my things and headed to college.

At college, I kept myself to myself once again, avoiding Andre and everyone else too. The day was a blur, but I'm sure I was there for the whole day. Clearly, it couldn't have been exciting in any shape or form.

When I arrived home that evening, Aunt Daiyu was already in.

"Wendy, is that you?" she asked.

"Yes Aunt Daiyu, it is," I replied, as I headed for the lounge.

Aunt Daiyu was watching the news.

"How was your day?" she asked.

"Same, same, just college I guess," I replied.

Aunt Daiyu smiled. As I was about to leave the lounge, she started talking again.

"Did you hear about the attack that was foiled last night?" asked Aunt Daiyu.

I panicked. How did she know, I thought to myself.

"Err, no, why, what happened?" I sheepishly asked.

"A girl was being attacked by two males. Out of nowhere, another girl appeared and saved her. The attackers got away," said Aunt Daiyu, rather excitedly.

"Really? Who was she?" I asked.

"No one saw her and she left no name. But if it hadn't been for her, the poor girl would definitely have ended up in hospital and who knows where else," replied Aunt Daiyu.

"It's all over the news at the moment," she added.

I turned to watch the news. A senior police officer was about to be interviewed.

"It was a very brave thing to do, however we must urge caution and advise against such actions in the future. We could be looking at two innocent girls being attacked. The right thing to do would be to call the police," said the police officer.

As soon as the police officer finished speaking, a reporter stood up and started to fire questions at him.

"Officer, do you have any leads as to who the girl was? What was she doing there? Is this the first time you have heard of her?" asked the reporter.

"At this stage, the girl is not being investigated and no, we do not know who she is or whether this is her first time. Thank you. No more questions for today," replied the police officer.

I was relieved. No one had seen me and my secret was safe.

"Call the police and they'll tell you that it's too late and they're doing all they can..." I said out loudly.

Aunt Daiyu looked towards me.

"I say good on her, whoever she is," as I shrugged off the conversation and headed upstairs.

I can still recall the inquisitive expression on Aunt Daiyu's face. Somehow deep down I felt she knew I had something to do with it.

That was the thing with elders, in that they had a sixth sense of their own and always knew when you were trying to hide something.

Let's just say that when it came to playing card games such as cheat, I was awful. They always managed to work me out and I'd lose each and every time.

Andre, Again…

The following day at college, I decided it was time to re-engage with Andre. Gosh, did I just say that? It sounded so formal.

What I meant to say was talk to Andre. It had been a while since we had a normal friendship, well, ever since the fire.

As I arrived at college, I headed to Bar Chocolato, Andre's usual pre-college hang out and just as I predicted, he was there.

"Hey," I said, as I approached him.

"Wendy, err, Hello!" replied Andre.

Andre was surprised, but in a pleasant way. I didn't need an invitation to join him. I simply pulled up a chair and sat down.

There was an awkward silence for a few seconds and then the conversation flowed about college life, the weather, in fact, everything and anything apart from the last few weeks.

I felt as though Andre was avoiding the topic on purpose. Only, I felt ready to talk about it and initiated the conversation.

"Andre, I just want to apologise for my behaviour over the last few weeks. I'm sorry for ignoring you. It's just that I…"

Andre sat up, reached for my hand and immediately interrupted me.

"Wendy, please stop. You have been through a terrible ordeal, with the fire and loss of both of your parents. You do not need to apologise. I'm sorry for what you have been through and I totally understand. I wish I could help answer your questions," replied Andre.

Even after being treated badly, Andre had no ill feeling towards me.

"I knew you needed time and space to deal with your loss and I had to respect that," added Andre.

Immediately, I felt a sharp pain and hurt inside me. I was missing my father. He was so right about Andre. He was so right about everything, just about all of the time except for sometimes!

"I was weak and should have handled it better. But my parents meant the world to me and the manner in which they left this world is something that I doubt I will ever come to terms with," I said.

Andre sighed. His eyes were fixed on me and he could sense how broken I was now.

"Sometimes in life we are faced with situations that truly test us as humans. We need to learn from these situations to better ourselves. Your loss has left a huge void in your life, but I'm sure that your parents are watching over you, following your every move with pride," said Andre.

"Thank you Andre. Thank you. I am trying, but it will take a while for me to let go. On some days, the feelings I have within me, let's just say that on those days, I don't think I can ever move on. There are too many unanswered questions in my life and that is what hurts me the most," I said, tearfully.

Andre told me that he understood, and to some extent he probably did.

"Wendy, just don't try to be a hero. Be yourself. Don't hold onto the anger and pain of what happened. In time, justice will be served to those that were responsible for this callous and hideous crime," said Andre.

"I'm trying, but it's not easy. My parents always taught me to respect the law and I have always done so," I replied.

I gathered my thoughts for a moment and sighed deeply.

"But, the police haven't done anything. They let the only witness leave as they felt that he was in the wrong place at the wrong time, that's all," I added.

"Time, Wendy, time. The police know what they are doing, even though at times they may not let on. You just have to give them time and be patient," replied Andre.

I did say that he was a straight talking law abiding citizen. There was no way that I could discuss what had happened the other day with him. He definitely would not approve and that was final.

What had started off as a general chat had turned into something quite emotional.

I felt very vulnerable, by being so open. Yet safe in the knowledge that Andre was not one to take advantage. To me, Andre was a very caring guy, not one to shy away from emotions. He tried to assure me that all was well and that it was normal for the police to take their time. In many ways, it was how the police worked, by keeping their cards close to their chest.

I felt that Andre seemed to have a better handle on my life and my ordeal than I did. Maybe this is what made him the person that he is. Maybe this is what my father saw in him and advocated that he was a good influence in my life. I knew that mentally he was very strong and that he was able to separate his actions from his emotions.

He demonstrated that he had strong family values too. Maybe I needed to learn more about his family in order to understand his reasoning at times.

Part of me wanted to open up more and tell him about my exploits, the anger that was inside me but I knew that it needed to remain a closely guarded secret.

Deep down, I wasn't convinced that he would be supportive of my actions and whether he would approve of the person that I was slowly becoming. If I'm being honest, I don't think he would ever side with me if I told him the truth.

As he did not talk about his family, especially his father, I felt that I couldn't just open up fully, not yet anyway.

I had to think about Andre. I couldn't just walk away from his friendship but at the same time, I couldn't fully embrace it.

I guess I needed to keep Andre very close now, but not close enough to allow him to share my secret. My secret needed to remain safe with me.

College Rumour Mill

The following day at college, there was a buzz of excitement in the air. Word about the attack on the young girl and more importantly the 'heroine' that had foiled the attack had spread quickly through the college.

Rumours had already started to circulate as to who it could be. Was it someone from our college? If so, who could it be? Early reports indicated that the girl was Caucasian with brown hair, whilst in other quarters it was alleged that she was Oriental with black hair.

I wasn't one for being the centre of attention and started to worry. What if the girl that I had helped recognised me? What if she was from the same college as me?

I thought I should divert attention from myself and I knew just the right place to achieve this.

I headed to the college cafeteria.

It was busy as usual, with just one empty table. I decided to go for a soft drink this time along with a chocolate chip cookie and headed for 'the' empty table.

I could feel many eyes on me at the cafeteria.

A few minutes passed and as expected, they turned up, Julie and Veronica, the college bullies.

"OMG! OMG! Girl, do you have a death wish?" said Veronica as she approached the table.

Julie laughed and then turned serious.

"Veronica, be careful, she might be the 'one', she looks weird enough!" said Julie, as she broke out into hysterical laughter.

They both looked at each other and then around the cafeteria at everyone else.

I decided to stand up in a rather authoritative manner and confront them. My peers were stunned. No doubt some of them were thinking that I might be the girl.

Yet, with a single push, Julie managed to knock me to the ground.

I was a little shaken, but once again, I decided to stand up.

This time, it was Veronica's turn as she also pushed me to the floor. As I fell, Julie reached for my bag and emptied it all over me.

Luckily, I wasn't seriously hurt.

As before, the cafeteria began to empty. I pretended to shed a tear as I started gathering my belongings. I was trying to act fast, whilst trying to create the illusion of fear. It seemed to be working perfectly.

Veronica moved around me and then behind me. She grabbed my hair and pulled my head back.

"Now, listen carefully. Next time you violate our space, you'll be in need of a lot of make-up in order to make your face look pretty again. Do I make myself clear?" shouted Veronica.

I nodded slowly, whilst pretending to sob. Once again, no one came to my aid or offered any assistance. It worked a treat.

Attention had been diverted away from me, convincing others that I too was just another ordinary girl.

As I picked up my belongings, I took a long hard look at both of them. I knew that their time would come one day. After all, someone needed to teach them a lesson.

Once You Start You Just Can't Stop

It was a few days later when I next decided to carve out some more chopsticks and then played with them.

On this occasion, I followed up the chopstick session with fifty intensive sit-ups, fifty leg raises and a selection of stretching exercises. This was so not me!

I recall having read about the perfect abs in a magazine article once and I just felt the urge to do the exercises. The adrenalin rush I experienced was immense and it felt so very right.

I wasn't a fitness fanatic. I was Wendy Wu and fitness wasn't part of my vocabulary.

Something was happening to me. I was changing and day-by-day I was becoming colder and more self-absorbed.

Now, it was all about me, me and me.

I was using the anger inside me to my advantage. I replayed the night that I saved the girl from being attacked, the thrill and excitement was second to none.

It was late at night and I decided to venture out once more. Luckily it wasn't raining on this occasion.

I walked for a while, on edge, looking for something, anything. In fact, I don't really know what I was looking for. I could feel anger building up inside me again. This time it was the news report that kept on replaying itself in my head. How the right thing to do would've been to call the police and let them do nothing about it. It also reminded me of the college bullies and how no one did anything about it, not once but on two separate occasions.

I didn't find the something that I was looking for and so I headed back home.

This became a regular pattern for a few days. I would just head out looking for something, maybe it was injustices or acts of crime that I was seeking and when I couldn't find anything, I would return home.

Day four and my patience paid off. I did experience the tingle down my spine, but as I was in the shower at the time, it didn't register and contributed it to the feeling of cold water running down my back.

Whilst out on one of my walks, I witnessed a crime. Two teenagers had managed to let themselves into a car. They were rummaging through the glove compartment when they noticed me.

"What are you looking at?" shouted one of them.

I remained calm and looked straight towards him. The second teenager emerged from inside the car.

"Maybe it's her car. Get the keys off her, let's take the car too," I heard him say.

"This is not your car and nor is it mine. You're committing a crime," I shouted.

They both turned towards each other and laughed. It was at that moment that I noticed their builds. They were very muscular.

"What? And you're going to stop us are you? You're in the wrong place girl," said one of them.

"At the wrong time," added the second teenager.

They both started to walk towards me. I could feel my heart pounding and the adrenalin rush kick in once again. But deep down, I was beginning to enjoy this feeling.

Here we go again, I thought to myself, only this time, I was better prepared. I quickly reached for the chopsticks and took aim at both teenagers.

I directly hit one of the teenagers in his chest, with such ferocity that he lost his balance and fell backwards onto the ground.

I threw a few more chopsticks straight at him, pinning him to the ground in the process. The chopsticks had pierced through his jeans.

I also hit the second teenager directly on his legs. But it wasn't enough and he charged towards me at speed. I didn't have sufficient time for another throw and had nowhere to run. Instead, I braced myself.

As he approached me, he dived towards me with a leaping tackle. Before I knew it, he had grabbed me by my waist and we went down in a heap. It was a painful landing, but luckily I wasn't seriously hurt.

He got on top of me, pulled out a knife and started waving it side to side in front of my face whilst telling me how he was going to draw pretty pictures on me. It looked like a very sharp knife. Why on earth would anyone carry a knife, I thought to myself.

I needed to defend myself and thought back to what my mother had taught me. It didn't seem like it was going to be sufficient as my assailant then reached for one of my chopsticks and pushed it towards me. I felt a scratch on my face. That hurt, I thought to myself, but my reaction was clear for him to see.

"The knife's going to feel even more painful," he commented, as he broke into laughter.

I started to struggle like a wild cat and rolled him off me, temporarily. Again, he leapt for me.

My fear turned to anger. In fact, I became very angry and in the process managed to wriggle my legs free, bending them whilst placing my feet on his chest.

I used all of my energy and the strength in my legs to push him off me. I was drained. A rush of adrenalin came to my aid. The leg exercises had certainly helped. I had surprised myself. Was this really me?

I felt energised and leapt for him, catching him by surprise as I landed on top of him. He was on the ground and didn't know what had hit him. I knew I had one chance and if I failed then I was in serious trouble.

As he shouted obscenities at me, I reached out for some chopsticks and stabbed them through his clothes. I skewered the chopsticks into the ground, first his right arm and then his left arm was pinned in a swift movement. With his arms secured, I ensured that his legs too were pinned down into the ground. He was left stunned.

I looked around and noticed his mobile phone on the floor beside him. I reached for it, with one goal in mind, to call the police.

He continued to yell abuse and insults towards me whilst trying to wriggle free, but I remained focussed. Seeing him like that made me smile. I don't know why, it just did.

"Police please…I have apprehended thieves on High Street, opposite Bank Square, come and get them," I said to the operator.

"Who is this? Can I have your name please?" replied the operator.

The operator started to ask me for more information.

I paused for a brief moment and then replied, "Justice is served," before throwing the phone to the ground.

I picked up my bag of chopsticks, looked around to make sure that I had everything and left the scene immediately, heading for home. I could hear sirens in the distance. Hopefully, it meant that the police were on the way.

I arrived home, ensuring that I was very careful as not to make any noise. Luckily, Aunt Daiyu was fast asleep. I headed straight upstairs and into the bathroom.

I quickly got undressed and stood under the shower, whilst enjoying the warmth from the hot water. I then noticed blood. It was the scratch on my cheek. It was a minor injury that I obtained during the scuffle that broke out. Instead of being upset, I simply smiled, quickly cleaned myself and finished my shower.

I dried myself, got changed and then headed to bed with a smile. I was very tired. It had been quite an eventful evening.

Surprisingly, there was only one feeling inside me and that wasn't one of fear. It was of excitement and a sense of satisfaction.

I had taken too many risks and was nearly caught. Next time, I needed to be more careful, I thought to myself.

Acceptance

It was Tuesday morning and Aunt Daiyu was awake before me for a change.

As I woke up I headed for the bathroom and decided to have a hot shower. I needed waking up. I loved the feeling of hot water on my head and flowing down my back. It felt invigorating. It was a quick shower as I didn't have much time, having slept in longer than usual.

When I started to dry myself, I noticed the scratch on my face. I kept calm and reached for my make-up. Hmm, concealer, perfect! I needed a few applications, but it worked a treat.

I got dressed and headed down for a quick breakfast.

"Morning," I said, as I entered the breakfast room.

"Good Morning Wendy. Sleep well?" asked Aunt Daiyu inquisitively.

"Yes Aunt Daiyu," I replied.

"How was your evening? Have fun?" she asked.

I knew something was wrong. Before I could answer, she continued.

"I noticed a few spots of blood in the hallway. Care to tell me what happened?"

I was stumped. How do I respond, I thought. And then I came out with the first thing that sprung to mind.

"I must've had a nose bleed, I don't know," I replied.

Aunt Daiyu wasn't impressed and knew that I wasn't being honest.

"Wendy, your parents taught you well. We do not lie to loved ones," she said in a raised voice.

"Why are you making such an issue of it? It's just a bit of blood," I replied.

Aunt Daiyu sighed, took a deep breath and shook her head.

"Wendy, I know of your secret. I know you are the girl that was mentioned in the news lately."

I was stunned. She knew of my secret!

"Wendy, I was awake at night and saw you come in," she added.

I had no answer to that although I had doubts as to whether she did actually see me. Instead, I insisted that I had been out with Andre, collected my belongings and headed for college.

My journey to college felt very long as fear crept inside me. What if Aunt Daiyu did see me? What if my secret was out? I tried to brush it off and occupied my mind with college.

There were days at college, which remained a blur. I guess they were rather run of the mill, on which nothing happened. I would just keep myself to myself.

As I arrived home from college that evening, I pretended that the disagreement we had in the morning, didn't happen. But Aunt Daiyu had other ideas.

I entered the lounge and noticed that Aunt Daiyu was holding one of my chopsticks in her hand.

"Hello Wendy, care to explain this?" she asked.

Immediately, I became defensive.

"You have no right to enter my room and go through my belongings!" I shouted.

Aunt Daiyu was not going to be deflected.

"Wendy, this morning I find blood stains in the hallway and on the stairs. I have also been watching the news," said Aunt Daiyu who then paused.

"The car thieves and the girl that was being attacked...the girl that helped," said Aunt Daiyu.

"Are you accusing me of something? It wasn't me!" I interrupted loudly.

Deep down, I knew that I had nowhere to hide anymore. She knew of my secret.

"I have noticed your behavioural changes lately, as well as the changes to your body shape," added Aunt Daiyu.

Sure enough, my behaviour had changed but it was my body changes that were more obvious. I had started to become more athletic and toned all over, even in the space of a few weeks.

"Well? Are you going to deny that it was you?" she asked again.

At this point I had nothing left to say. I looked at her and slowly started to lose control. Tears began to flow. Aunt Daiyu walked over towards me and immediately put her arms around me.

"Wendy, Wendy, Wendy...Why?" asked Aunt Daiyu soothingly.

"Justice needs to be served for my parents. I can't sit there as though nothing has ever happened. My parents were murdered," I replied.

Aunt Daiyu didn't say a word. Instead she just held me tightly.

I was confused and didn't know how to react. I sat down with Aunt Daiyu and we had dinner together. I felt that I had let Aunt Daiyu down. I felt upset, confused and really missed my parents.

As we were having dinner, Aunt Daiyu opened up. She started by telling me how inquisitiveness had got the better of her whilst I was at college and so she decided to enter my room.

She told me that as she entered, she noticed that the poster on the wardrobe was almost peeling off. A few days ago, the same poster was on the bedroom wall. Her intention was to stick the poster back on when she noticed the holes in the wardrobe door. On closer inspection, she realised there was more to them than she envisaged.

She then started looking around my room and after several minutes, she found what she was looking for. It was a broken chopstick that was lying underneath my wardrobe.

She paused and then sighed before she went on to explain how she started to link it all to me.

As she picked up the chopstick for closer inspection, she had a flashback. It was the news article, which featured the young girl in the foiled attack. There was a mention of sticks being used. She switched on the television and waited patiently for my return.

On the midday news, the headlines featured a story about car thieves that had been operating in the area for the last few months. They had finally been caught. However, it was when the reporter mentioned a girl at the scene that Aunt Daiyu took note.

"A girl apprehended the thieves whilst they were in the middle of a robbery. Reports indicate that a scuffle broke out and somehow the girl overpowered the thieves. Both were found pinned into the ground with what looks like sticks," said the reporter.

"Police are sending a strong message to this girl. Whilst we are grateful for your help, you will get hurt. Please leave the job of catching criminals to the professionals," added the senior police officer.

Aunt Daiyu explained she was in no doubt anymore. She was convinced that it was me that was behind these incidents and felt that she needed to intervene before I got hurt.

I sat there quietly and ate my dinner. What response could I possibly give her?

After dinner, I helped Aunt Daiyu clear the dishes, before heading off to my bedroom.

I couldn't sleep straight away, as my mind was buzzing. I thought about the previous nights and the two incidents. Was I wrong to help the girl that was being attacked? Was I wrong to prevent the car thieves from taking something that was not theirs?

I was confused. In my head, I knew I had done the right thing. Yet in my heart, I felt an emptiness and sadness. I was not one to let down family.

In fact, in all my years, I had never once let down my parents and yet I had felt that I had let Aunt Daiyu down.

I started crying, curled up and slowly drifted to sleep.

Outfit for a Misfit

The following day, I returned home from college earlier than usual as one of my lessons had been cancelled. Instead of spending it at college, I thought it would be good to perhaps spend it with Aunt Daiyu.

However, I was not very happy. As I walked in to my room, I noticed a pair of black leggings on the floor outside my wardrobe. Aunt Daiyu had clearly been in my room again. I simply knew she had as I hadn't worn that pair for a few days and I always tidied up my room.

The front door opened and Aunt Daiyu walked in. She seemed to be in a hurry.

I quickly ran downstairs to meet her. As I entered the lounge, I just stood there with my arms folded.

"Aunt Daiyu! You've been in my room again!" I shouted.

Aunt Daiyu dropped her bags and headed towards me.

"What were you doing in my room? You talk about trust and honesty and supporting me and then you rummage through my things!" I added, whilst holding the pair of leggings in my hand, which Aunt Daiyu clearly had forgotten to put back.

Aunt Daiyu reached for my hand, but I immediately pulled away. I was absolutely livid. How was this any different to the discussion we had last night? I had cried myself to sleep thinking that I had let her down.

"Wendy, you need to start trusting me more. I am not your enemy but completely with you, supportive in every way," replied Aunt Daiyu.

"You are all I have in life and I am not about to give up on you. I have a sense of responsibility towards you, in more ways than one," she added.

"Then what were you doing in my room? Why were you going through my belongings?" I asked.

"Come with me," replied Aunt Daiyu, as she took me by her hand and headed to the spare room.

As we entered, I truly gasped. I was stunned, and in complete disbelief. Aunt Daiyu had been working on an outfit for me.

"Wendy, for you, my love, after all, every misfit needs an outfit," whispered Aunt Daiyu.

I was rooted to the spot and overcome with emotion.

"It's beautiful. It's..." I whispered.

"Wendy, the path you have chosen is a dangerous one and you must be protected, especially your identity. Now do you believe in me?" asked Aunt Daiyu.

I nodded and smiled. I didn't know what else to say or do. It was totally unexpected and very surreal. I needed to pinch myself to check I was not dreaming.

"May I try it on?" I asked.

Aunt Daiyu reached for the outfit and gently passed it over to me. It felt amazingly soft and looked very professional, surely not something that had been made at home.

"Aunt Daiyu, where did you get this from?" I asked.

"I made it especially for you my dear, hence needing to look through your wardrobe," replied Aunt Daiyu.

I didn't know how to react. I was genuinely lost for words.

"Now that I have made it, please, let me see you in it," asked Aunt Daiyu.

I slowly headed to my room and got changed, after which I stood in front of the mirror and smiled. It was elegant and sophisticated. She even managed to make it using my favourite colours. That explained why she was in my room. I felt guilty for shouting at her earlier.

I headed back into the spare room to Aunt Daiyu.

"You will need these too," said Aunt Daiyu, as she gave me a pair of boots that she had just bought from Grand Central.

As I sat down to put on the boots, Aunt Daiyu walked over towards me and started to caress my hair, reaching for a hairbrush and some chopsticks in the process. I sat patiently as Aunt Daiyu finished off what she was doing.

"Come, stand up and let's look at you now," said Aunt Daiyu as she helped me towards the mirror.

"Now that looks perfect. You're trending on social media and already seem to have a cult following. So, it's only fair that we gave the world a new heroine," said Aunt Daiyu.

As I looked in the mirror I felt a tingle throughout my body. I loved the hair and the use of chopsticks to keep it in place. My look was complete. Was that really me? Was that really Wendy Wu?

"We need to think about a mask too. Hmm, let me see what I can do," said Aunt Daiyu.

This was surreal. Aunt Daiyu was supporting the path that I had chosen to follow without even discussing it with me or even trying to understand what my intentions were.

Aunt Daiyu explained how she had set herself a target. As soon as I left for college, she entered my room and decided to explore my wardrobe. It wasn't a huge task as I had lost all of my clothes in the fire and had to rebuild it completely.

"Pastels, pinks and blacks are what you seem to like," said Aunt Daiyu.

I simply nodded and Aunt Daiyu continued.

"Wendy, your wardrobe contained a blend of semi-casual and formal clothes. I picked out a few clothes and inspected them, whilst making a note of the sizes. I then headed to look at your footwear collection," she added.

That couldn't have taken long at all, as I was down to just three pairs.

"I then tidied your room and left it as I found it. Well, clearly I didn't as otherwise I would've put the leggings back!" she said, smiling.

Once Aunt Daiyu was committed to a cause, she was all in, definitely Miss One Hundred Percent.

"I then headed to my room, reached for a sheet of paper, a pencil and got to work, creativity in hand. After an hour, I paused and reached for some coloured pencils, in order to apply the finishing touches," she went on to add.

She then explained how she finished with her creation and held it up with a sense of pride.

She had clearly decided that I needed an outfit. Luckily, she was the creative type and was a dab hand when it came to sewing.

As she passed over the illustration to me, I became tearful. There I was, or rather an illustration of me. I was wearing a pink jacket, with a belt, complete with black leggings and a pair of black knee high boots.

To finish off, she decided it would be best if my hair was worn up, and kept in place with a pair of chopsticks.

"Once I had the design, I headed upstairs to the spare room, where I kept my sewing machine and supplies. I reached for a pink fabric roll and a pair of scissors and got to work. After a short while, I reached for the roll of black stretch fabric, perfect for leggings. Again, I got to work with my scissors," smiled Aunt Daiyu.

She was a dab hand when it came to using scissors too. Above all, Aunt Daiyu was a very focussed and determined individual.

"It took me a few hours to make it. I felt proud when I had finished it and was very happy with myself. I then headed downstairs, grabbed my coat, bag, and keys and headed out to Grand Central," said Aunt Daiyu.

"Why did you need to go there?" I asked.

She explained that she headed for the shoe shops, browsing from one to another until she found what she was looking for, black stretch knee high boots in a size six. She did know me very well.

"Wendy, I was hoping to be back before you so that I could set up a surprise and avoid any confrontation with you," said Aunt Daiyu whilst looking at me.

I felt upset. She had done so much and tried so hard to create this and yet I had hit out at her. I was amazed, surprised and confused at the speed at which Aunt Daiyu had managed to create the outfit.

The Box

Part of me was still confused. How could a homemade chopstick become so powerful and be used as a weapon?

From the first time I suggested making them, my father showed a keen interest and was quick to help me. He sourced the wood for me, emphasizing that it was 'sacred wood' that had been blessed.

"Aunt Daiyu, how can these chopsticks be so powerful? I have managed to pin down grown men with them. What is it about them?" I asked.

"Father said something about sacred wood?" I added.

Aunt Daiyu looked at me and sighed. It was as though she knew the answer but at first was very reluctant to answer.

"The wood is from special trees that grow in Zhejiang. We believe that the trees are blessed and are in the world to protect us," replied Aunt Daiyu.

And then she paused, almost as though she was choosing to be selective with her answers. I felt that she was doing this a lot lately, in terms of telling me bits that she felt I needed to know, without telling me everything.

"But, Wendy, it is not just about the chopsticks. It's about you as well," she added.

Aunt Daiyu then disappeared for a few minutes before returning with a long jade box. It looked very old. It was engraved in mandarin text and included a number of Chinese symbols on the sides. It was a relic.

"Wendy, for you, my love," said Aunt Daiyu as she handed me the box.

"What is it?" I asked.

"Your destiny. Open it and see," replied Aunt Daiyu.

I opened the box and didn't know how to react.

It was a pair of shiny chopsticks. They were beautiful and I had never seen anything like them in my life.

"Wendy, the chopsticks are made from silver and are diamond tipped. Be careful, they can pierce through anything. They are very tough and you must use them wisely," said Aunt Daiyu as she smiled.

"Aunt Daiyu, where did you get these from? I don't know what to say..." I said, quietly.

"In time, I will tell you everything you need to know about these and why I am entrusting you with them, but not now," replied Aunt Daiyu.

"Wendy, you must learn to control your anger. When anger rises, think of the consequences," said Aunt Daiyu.

I had heard that before many times, from my father. Did she read the same book of quotes, I thought to myself.

My father would quite often quote Confucius as he had a quote for every situation. And most of the quotes, well, you couldn't argue with them. Aunt Daiyu wasn't far behind.

"Wendy, there are three principles that you must adhere to. These are as follows:

One: You must never be caught.

Two: You must always detach yourself
            from emotion.

Three: You must always remain true to
          yourself. Purity.

Always remember these, especially in your darkest hour," she added.

That seemed to be a very deep and meaningful message. I remember my father mentioning purity and always remaining true to myself. In fact, it was on my sixteenth birthday when he last mentioned that, just before he made me drink a glass of ice-cold water, claiming that it was blessed. Then again, for as long as I can remember, it's happened at every birthday.

Aunt Daiyu was present on that day. I figured that she must know something about that ritual.

Today wasn't the day to question her. I wanted to ask her everything. I needed to know everything. But, Aunt Daiyu clearly felt that I wasn't ready for everything. I had to believe in her, as no doubt she had my best interests at heart.

The simplicity of the principles was a sign of the relationship that I would end up forming with Aunt Daiyu. In many ways, it was a binding contract of trust between us. I needed to respect that and use it to build trust between us so that perhaps she could open up and reveal more to me.

With Aunt Daiyu on my side, I was ready for the world now. Hopefully the world was ready for me.

Time to Work

It was a very emotional day for me, after Aunt Daiyu had presented me with the outfit. I realised that I could trust her with everything and no longer be afraid of how she would react.

We sat down and had dinner together. Aunt Daiyu had made steamed sea bass in a Szechuan sauce served with vegetables and steamed baby potatoes. You could say it was a semi-fusion dish. As we ate our dinner, we chatted away like we once used to. It was nice, relaxing and refreshing.

As we both rose to clear the table and prepare for the dessert course, it happened again. I felt a shiver shoot down my spine and a tingling sensation throughout my body. It was definitely as though I had developed a sixth sense only, it was for all things bad.

"Aunt Daiyu, it's happening again. It's that feeling I experienced on the night my parents were killed and to a lesser extent, the two incidents I was involved in," I said.

Aunt Daiyu put down her dishes and looked towards me.

"What is it? What are you experiencing or sensing?" asked Aunt Daiyu.

"I don't know, but I have a feeling that something bad is about to happen. I have just had an image of the bank in the old square rush through my head and the sight of money. This has never happened before. It's almost as though my powers are developing," I replied.

Aunt Daiyu hesitated and then smiled.

"I think it's time for you to go to work, don't you?" asked Aunt Daiyu.

I smiled, put down the dishes that I had been carrying and dashed upstairs to get changed.

It was probably the quickest I have ever changed outfits. I put on my new boots and headed downstairs. Aunt Daiyu quickly styled my hair and then used a black strip of cloth to improvise and create a mask before handing it to me.

I felt overwhelmed but ready in so many ways. I thought back to some of the movies I had seen about heroes and I felt inspired. I was ready to kick butt!

Aunt Daiyu insisted on driving me to the old square and in some ways watch over me.

As we headed to the garage, I was dumbstruck. She had managed to get the entire car windows tinted. When did she do that? Boy was she serious about this 'project'!

We arrived near the old square and I got out of the car, making sure that no one had seen me.

"Good luck!" said Aunt Daiyu, as she grasped both of my hands.

I headed off on foot to the back of the old square towards the bank, to the same area that I had seen in the vision that flashed through my head.

It was deserted and there was no one there. Was I too late, I asked myself? Were my senses way off the mark? What if I had misjudged things and got everything wrong? Many doubts started to enter my mind.

Was there a bank robbery? If so, how come there was no alarm? I climbed up scaffolding on the side of the building opposite the bank and found a place on the roof from where I could see the bank.

And then, it happened. I heard footsteps in the street below, so I knelt down, in anticipation of what was to follow.

Time to Reflect

The last thirty minutes were a blur.

My heart was still racing as the adrenalin slowly started to ebb away. I am sure you remember what had just happened, as I looked down from the roof at the aftermath of my actions.

I felt a sense of pride as I saw the perpetrators of the crime being apprehended by the police. Justice.

It was then that I realised that there was no street lighting. The power must have been taken out. I looked around and it seemed pretty dark. I guess I didn't need to worry about CCTV!

I climbed down from the building and walked away, making sure that no one was following me. I walked to the side street where Aunt Daiyu had parked and quickly got in her car.

"Are you ok?" asked Aunt Daiyu.

"Yes. Justice is served to a group of bank robbers," I replied.

Aunt Daiyu smiled and replied, "Let's go home."

"Thank you for my outfit. I feel more confident out there now and have no fear inside me," I replied.

I took off my mask and cleaned my face with a soft wipe. Aunt Daiyu acknowledged my comment with a smile and drove us home. I could see the glimmer of pride in her eyes. She was full of raw emotion too.

"Wendy, you're hurt. We need to get that seen to and give you a little more protection out there," said Aunt Daiyu.

I had been injured during the scuffles that broke out and needed to treat my cuts. Today was the first time that I had seriously hurt anyone. With the earlier assailants that I faced, I merely pinned them down, ensuring that the chopsticks went through their clothes, thus avoiding the body completely. I knew that there would be times where I would need to use even more force. Today was that day and Aunt Daiyu was right; the chopsticks were very sharp.

I knew I needed to increase the intensity of my exercise routines to ensure my body remained in shape. To others this could simply be attributed to the fact that I was a female obsessed with her body shape and size, with peer influences from college kicking in. I was never really into exercise but something inside me really had changed.

For a start, I thought back to the few encounters that I had and how I managed to overcome the situations. Things could so easily have gone against me. I needed to ensure that I was always in control and to never be in a situation that I could not handle. With the path that I was choosing to follow, I knew that would be difficult.

Aunt Daiyu vowed to make a few improvements to my outfit, including my mask, to ensure that my identity could never be worked out. She knew best and I decided that I would no longer challenge her.

I had a confidant, an ally and someone to look over me now. I guess I was ready for the next step.

The Revelation

I was curious and my curiosity was getting the better of me.

Aunt Daiyu was very supportive of the path that I was choosing to follow and demonstrating levels of care and understanding beyond belief.

We had both suffered recently and our loss could never be truly quantified. Yet, Aunt Daiyu was always one to live a life following the straight path and not one for wanting to fall foul of the law.

Here she was, choosing to be my best friend, whilst also taking up legal responsibilities for me.

It is said that blood is thicker than water and here I was, witnessing it in action.

I was proud, proud of the family values that had been instilled in me.

"Aunt Daiyu, why do you choose to support me rather than scold me for my actions and the path that I am following?" I asked.

Aunt Daiyu smiled and turned towards me.

"Wendy, I am surprised it has taken you so long to ask me, when that question has probably been on your mind from the minute I first helped you," replied Aunt Daiyu.

"You are blessed with ability, vision and the determination to succeed in life. You have the mental willpower to overcome all obstacles in life. You are a Wu," Aunt Daiyu went on to add.

At that moment, I recalled the words of my father and shed a tear.

'Our greatest glory is not in never falling, but in rising every time we fall.'

I became emotional at the thought of what my father would have said and shed a tear.

I let out a huge sigh, headed for the nearest chair and sat down. I was feeling emotional and confused. I lifted my feet up, wrapped my arms around my legs and sat there rocking.

So many thoughts entered my mind.

"Wendy, there is something that I need to share with you. Something about your parents, the truth about what probably happened," said Aunt Daiyu in a soft voice, as she headed towards me.

My parents had been killed in a fire, which started as a result of a robbery that had gone wrong. At least that's what the police had told me.

I sat up, wiped my eyes and looked straight at my aunt.

"Wendy, I believe that your parents were targeted deliberately," she said.

There was no immediate reaction from me.

"They were receiving threats, unwarranted threats," added Aunt Daiyu.

I could sense the anger inside me growing again and I was struggling to contain myself. Aunt Daiyu never mentioned anything about this before, not even to the police.

"How can you say such a thing? What is it that you know?" I asked.

"You have every right to be angry, but please, try to understand, we have been trying to protect you," replied Aunt Daiyu.

I started to shake my head.

"No, no, no, no, no! How dare you say you were protecting me!" I screamed.

Aunt Daiyu walked over towards me and hugged me. As I tried to push her away, her grip became tighter. She kissed me on my head and sighed.

I was angry and I could no longer contain myself. Tears were flowing uncontrollably from my eyes and my whole body started to tremble.

Aunt Daiyu used her hands to wipe my tears away whilst holding my face.

"Wendy, I know you're angry and you have every right to be feeling that way. I promised your parents that

I would never tell you the truth, but I can no longer keep this from you. I have never broken a promise before," said Aunt Daiyu, as she too began to cry.

So here we were, two emotional wrecks, the only family we had.

I looked up towards my aunt and spoke, "Why? Why?" I asked, sobbing uncontrollably.

"It all began in Zhejiang and it played a huge part in their decision to leave. I guess their past finally caught up with them," said Aunt Daiyu as she started to share their story.

"The elderly gentleman at the funeral, did he have something to do with this?" I asked.

"Yes...maybe...probably...he may have been one of them," replied Aunt Daiyu.

One of...? I thought to myself. I needed to know more. Something didn't add up.

"Wendy, no, not today. Not today. Please? Not today," said Aunt Daiyu as tears flowed down her face.

She sobbed uncontrollably with the occasional "I'm sorry Wendy, I'm sorry. I thought I could tell you, but now I am not sure."

I was no closer to understanding who, what, why, but I knew, that my initial instinct was correct that there was more to the fire than what I was led to believe. I just held her close to me for a few minutes until she was ready.

"Wendy, your actions lately, your unselfish nature, the strength and determination you have displayed, all of this has given me the strength to open up my heart to you," said Aunt Daiyu.

And then I finally drew up the courage to ask her for the first time.

"Uncle?" I asked rather sheepishly.

Aunt Daiyu looked a little startled and then she spoke.

"Yes...he is in Zhejiang, so I am led to believe," replied Aunt Daiyu.

I had no response to that at all. Finally after all these years, I was being let into the family secret or getting an insight into it. For a start, it explained why Aunt Daiyu had never remarried. Uncle Li was still alive.

I was motionless and simply overcome with raw emotion. Once again, I had more questions than answers. I had to accept that this would continue to be the case until I found those responsible for my parents death.

"First, we must grow stronger, together. You, my angel, have much to learn," said Aunt Daiyu.

"But, you are pure and the use of chopsticks to serve justice is a wise fusion. We need to work on the appetisers and dessert," she added, as she tried to make me smile.

"Wendy...this is your destiny. This is what your mother would've wanted," added Aunt Daiyu.

"But, I thought my parents wanted me to study and realise my career aspirations?" I asked.

"I thought my parents were happy about me following a career as a lawyer? It was fathers idea that I reach for the stars and aim to have my own law firm," I added.

"Yes, Wendy. Your father was supportive of you realising your career aspirations. He was always one for staying on the right side of the law, remember?" replied Aunt Daiyu.

"But...then...?" I stuttered.

"Your destiny is your destiny. There is nothing stopping you from following your dreams. But your destiny is also to 'serve and protect'," replied Aunt Daiyu.

Serve and protect? That sounded like a motto for the police!

And so it began. From that day on, Aunt Daiyu became my guide and a tower of strength in more ways that I could ever have imagined.

Little was I to know that Aunt Daiyu had a lot more secrets, which would become known to me soon. But, that I would save for another time.

I was intrigued and aching to hear more about my parents 'murders'.

I knew that I had begun the next stage of my journey, one that would no doubt take me on many adventures.

Patience was never my strongest point, but, I was always told, 'It does not matter how slowly you go, so long as you do not stop'.

I needed to be patient and take slow steady steps in order to reach the next destination.

Betrayal

It was the weekend and time to relax. Aunt Daiyu and I had decided to spend the day together.

After a light lunch, we headed to Grand Central to shop. Neither of us needed anything, but since when do us girls need an excuse to shop!

It was nice just spending time with my aunt without thinking about anything else for a change. In many ways, it allowed us both to just escape from reality for a short period of time.

There were a number of new shops that had recently opened as well as a major department store. We decided that we needed to fully explore every new shop before setting each other a challenge. It was something that I regularly did with my mother.

I wanted to buy Aunt Daiyu a new outfit as a way to thank her for just being there and she too felt the same about me. So, we gave each other two hours to shop for each other after which we would meet at the Grand Central café.

Aunt Daiyu lacked confidence in herself lately and I wanted to help rebuild that. I decided to give her a full makeover. I headed to the department store.

As I arrived, an emerald dress immediately caught my eye. It was a fishtail dress with an elegant printed pattern and a figure hugging fit. It was stunning. I knew Aunt Daiyu loved green and she definitely had the figure to carry it off, plus this dress definitely oozed class and that summed up my aunt.

I rummaged through the handrail for her size. Luckily, there was one size ten dress left, perfect!

Next up, I needed a pair of shoes or rather an elegant pair of shoes and knew just the shop. Remember, I am an expert when it came to shoes and it helped that Aunt Daiyu has the same foot size as me.

An hour and a half had passed by very quickly and I was almost done. Not being content with my purchases,

I decided to pick up some accessories, or rather, elegant earrings and a matching necklace for completeness.

The two hours were up and I was done. It had been a long, long time since I had so much fun, away from all of life's stresses.

I headed to the Grand Central café. Aunt Daiyu was waiting outside patiently. She was smiling and that made me smile. I hadn't seen her truly smile in months, apart from the brief moment that I tried on the outfit she had made.

We headed into the café, ordered two hot chocolates, two slices of chocolate cheesecake and sat down to discuss our shopping. It was just the best time we both had in a very long while. Both outfits matched our personalities to a tee. I guess it was an accurate reflection of just how well we knew each other.

It was the perfect cue for Aunt Daiyu to just randomly open up.

"Betrayal. That's what it's all about, betrayal and power. Your mother was a very, very special woman," said Aunt Daiyu.

I was taken back and my smile and laughter was gone.

"Aunt Daiyu?" I said in a soft voice.

"Yes Wendy, I can no longer keep secrets from you. You have made me smile again and revitalised me in every way," replied Aunt Daiyu.

"Your father was betrayed by his eldest brother, your uncle. An uncle you never knew you had. Jealousy got the better of him, I guess. Your mother...she was an incredibly pious women and one that was blessed. She was a princess and a guardian of the City of Jade, a sacred shrine, which is full of treasures. It contains the Well of the Jade Dragon," added Aunt Daiyu.

She looked towards me for a reaction, but there wasn't one.

"It is believed that if you drink from the Well of the Jade Dragon, you are bestowed a sixth sense. Your mind and body experience heightened sensations. You are able to utilise your brain to a much higher capacity than ordinary humans and are able to push your body further too," said Aunt Daiyu.

I was shocked and confused.

"But what has this got to do with anything?" I asked.

"Your parents left China when it became known that your mother was a guardian. Your uncle betrayed your father. He wanted to extract the location of the City of Jade and all of its secrets from your mother. Your father had no other option but to escape, hence they left Zhejiang and arrived here," said Aunt Daiyu.

As she paused for breath, she shed a tear.

"Your Uncle Li was captured. Your uncle hoped that your father would help save his brother in law. But they always vowed to one another that your mother's secret would remain intact. To this date, I am led to believe that he is still being held captive," said Aunt Daiyu tearfully.

She was clearly emotional, but this was some revelation. Talk about having a dark family secret.

"Earlier, you told me that the elderly Chinese gentleman from the funeral might be involved. Who are they?" I asked.

"They belong to a secret society called the Chi's. They have devoted their lives to finding and seizing the ancient relics of the City of Jade," she replied.

"The triangular shaped dragon symbol?" I asked.

"Yes...that is the symbol of the Chi's," replied Aunt Daiyu.

Colour had faded from her face. I knew she was finding this very difficult.

It was the same symbol that I had seen on the survivor from the fire and the bank robbers. The Chi's were clearly a force to be reckoned with.

"Over the last few months, your parents started receiving threatening phone calls and visits from their members. At first your parents denied that they knew anything or that they were the Wu's that the Chi's had been seeking, until your father was shown a photo of your uncle. After witnessing the shock on his face, they knew they were the ones," replied Aunt Daiyu.

"Your mother would have been able to protect both her and your father but she had a mortal fear of uncontrolled fire. It was her Achilles heel and they must have known that," she added.

Fire? Achilles heel? How would my mother have been able to protect both my father and her? What was this all about?

"But, what did they want? Why kill my parents?" I asked.

Aunt Daiyu held my hand tightly, gazed into my eyes and took another deep breath.

"Your mother had kept some water from the Well of the Jade Dragon, but she gave the last of this to you on your sixteenth birthday, which you might recall," said Aunt Daiyu.

"The ritual on my sixteenth birthday? Is that why I now get the tingling feeling whenever I sense something bad is about to happen?" I asked.

"Yes, but you will need to channel your energies and learn to understand the difference between good and bad," replied Aunt Daiyu.

Now it started to make sense. I had many questions, but slowly they were beginning to be answered.

"In time you will learn about the City of Jade and the duties that have been bestowed upon you as you too are a guardian. Only I know your destiny and in time I will share mine, but not today. I made a vow to your parents that if ever anything happened, I would look after you and one day tell you everything, but only if you were ready. We have so much to achieve together," said Aunt Daiyu.

Realising that this was a significant moment in my life, she took my hand and grasped it tightly.

"This is just the beginning," added Aunt Daiyu.

She was right. I had a lot to take in. It's not every day that you're told that you're a guardian of the City of Jade, right? My head was all over the place. Some of it made sense, but the rest of it was unreal. It was like a huge riddle unravelling before me.

We collected our bags and headed home.

During the journey home, so many things went through my head. At the forefront of my thoughts was justice for my parents and freeing Uncle Li. Then there was the City of Jade and the Well of the Jade Dragon, wherever that was.

And then it hit me. What about the Chi's? What if all of a sudden they targeted Aunt Daiyu or me?

It all now started to make sense as to why Aunt Daiyu was so supportive of my actions over the last few weeks. We needed to protect ourselves.

Change

As we arrived home, I headed straight to my room. I guess I just needed some me time now.

I unpacked the shopping and put the clothes away. I was feeling agitated and for once, my room looked messy. I decided to just tidy everything up. My head was all over the place, after all, there was a lot to take in. So many questions had been answered but I'm not sure I was ready for all of the answers I was given.

Aunt Daiyu had stopped by twice, but I hardly noticed, I was in my own world. I didn't know where to start and how to piece everything together.

A lot had happened in my life over the last few months. I started to think about my first day at college through to the fire and funeral. Losing my parents was something that almost broke me. Yet, somehow I had to hold it together. Now I knew why.

My body has undergone so much change lately and as for my senses well I'm not sure if I truly understood them anymore. I felt more alert about my surroundings and all those around me. And then there was that feeling, the feeling that something bad was about to happen. Was I ready for so much responsibility? What if I was unable to help when I get the 'call'?

More importantly, just where did my responsibilities lie and why me? There isn't even a rulebook or manual to read.

Before today, I was just an ordinary college girl, not wanting to be at the centre of attention and wanting to just live an ordinary life. Now, I didn't know who I was.

My father always spoke about right and wrong, good and bad. In fact, it was something he once wrote on a piece of paper, which he left in my bag. He was always doing that when he wanted to teach me positivity. I keep all of his messages in my handbag. Here it is:

'It is easy to hate and is difficult to love. That is how the whole scheme of things works. All good things are difficult to achieve and bad things are very easy to get'.

The reality was that for now, it was easy to hate and not to love.

I was always taught to follow the path of good and no matter what to never deviate from this path. Father always said that it was my destiny. Now I know why my father kept drilling that into me.

In college I had witnessed at first hand that people did not want to stand up against wrongs, even when they were happening in front of them. But here I was, with a very different mindset.

My mother always taught me to be very ladylike but there was a part of her that was always willing me to be a winner. I still remember my sixteenth birthday and the message she gave me, which was 'The will to win, the desire to succeed, the urge to reach your potential these are the keys that will unlock the door to personal excellence'.

Both of my parents wanted me to be the best at everything that I did and they never once wanted me to settle for anything less. Now when I try to look back, it's as though they were in many ways preparing me for this, my destiny.

My outlook on life, my mindset, and behaviour, everything about me needed to change. In fact, parts of it had already started to change.

Great responsibility had been bestowed upon me and I needed to rise to the challenge. Somehow, I had to grow up very quickly and a new me needed to evolve from this simple college girl that I was.

I stopped what I was doing for a moment and noticed a figure in the doorway. It was Aunt Daiyu. She had been standing there for a while, just watching me.

I looked over towards her and smiled. I didn't know what else to do. She too in turn looked towards me and smiled. In fact, we just stared at each other for a few minutes. I felt a strong connection towards her. And then she spoke.

"You're not alone Wendy, you're not alone," said Aunt Daiyu.

I smiled and nodded my head. Deep down, I knew that I wasn't alone, but that wasn't a great help at this moment in time. I somehow had to learn to deal with the change in my life. I had to learn how to channel my energies in the right way.

Everything changed today and in many ways, I guess I had no other choice but to come of age.

Who am I?

Self-fulfilment. Some regard it as being an egotistic, selfish and self-centred concept, impossible to achieve. But I didn't see it that way. I was working towards self-fulfilment and it was dependent upon my ability to fully exploit the potential that was trapped inside me.

I recalled my fathers words once again, 'Wherever you go, go with all your heart'. They couldn't be more appropriate than at this moment in my life.

I now had a new direction in life.

If father were here, he would be looking towards Confucius for words of wisdom, 'To see what is right, and not to do it, is want of courage'.

I had the courage to do what I felt was right, undoing the wrongs of others.

I was keeping my father close to me at all times, turning to Confucius when I needed inspiration. My father always said to 'study the past if you would define the future'.

I made this a part of my life, learning from my past mistakes in order to better myself.

I used this as an inspiration to also learn about my parents past as I knew that this too would define my future.

I needed to keep a balance between the two lives that I was living, ensuring that I appeared to be the model student in college, living a simple life. I had started to build my circle of friends now, which included Andre, Lucinda and Tara.

We all have dreams and aspirations in life. I too was no different. However, I needed to realign some of my priorities. I wanted to avenge my parents 'murder' and bring those responsible to justice. But this meant that I needed to take small steady steps.

This city needs me to help those in fear. I also need to understand more about my role as a guardian of the City of Jade. I know that there is much more to come. More adventures, more risks, more challenges and a lot more secrets to be revealed.

When I look at myself in the mirror, I no longer see Wendy Wu. Instead, I see someone more courageous.

I see someone who wants to make the world a better, safer place for one and all. I see someone who wants to challenge and stand up to the wrongs that are being committed in life today. I see someone who is no longer governed by the fantasy of a prince charming sweeping her off her feet. This someone needs a new identity, a new name to go with the new outfit.

And so, I was created and introduced to this great city of mine.

Who am I?

I am Chopstix. Justice will be served...